The Young Partisans

A Time Travel Adventure in WWII Poland

Book One of the *Heirs of the Candle Series*

Donna B. Gawell

Blendon Woods Press

Photos of the main characters and historic photos of the region during WWII can be found on the author's website.

www.DonnaGawell.com

The Young Partisans/Donna B. Gawell. -- 1st edition.

ISBN: 9798739875457
Imprint: Independently published

This book is dedicated to Colin, Elise, and Naomi. If they had lived through WWII in Poland, they surely would have been as brave as their ancestors who served in Poland's Home Army.

A Gromnica or "Thunder Candle"

Chapter One

The Gromnica

Elise had never been afraid of a little rain, but the mutter of thunder in the distant blackened sky reminded her of a terrifying storm when she was only four. She and Colin spent most of that long-ago night in the basement of her grandparents' home and had seen the damage all around the city the next morning. Images of toppled poles and trees were burned into Elise's memory, leaving her with a healthy fear of wind and lightning.

"When will Mom and Dad get home from your parent-teacher conference?" Elise asked. "I'm worried about them."

Clicking through the channels, her thirteen-year-old brother finally found the Columbus Crew's game. "Don't worry—we've lived through lots of storms."

While Colin slouched on the couch to watch the soccer game, their dogs, Noah and Leia, nervously paced, circling it. "What? The game's been delayed because of the storm coming through!" Colin's eyes remained on the TV screen as he witnessed the pandemonium in the stadium. "Wow, the players and people are running out of the stadium!"

"Okay, this is getting scary! I'm going to call Mom and Dad and get them to come home right now." As he knelt next to Elise and the dogs, he dialed their dad's phone and waited. "Nothing, no dial tone. Nothing."

Through the back window, Elise watched as a spider's web of white lines blanketed the sky. "There's no rain coming down, only zig-zaggy lines of lightning," Elise said in a quavering voice, as her eyes misted and her chin quivered. "You know, our lights could go out just like at Grandma and Papa's house." As if on cue, the lights flickered, and they were plunged into darkness. The solitary security flashlight dimly illuminated a tiny corner of the room. "What do we do now, Colin?"

As the two sat huddled on the sofa with Leia on Elise's lap, Noah, their Great Pyrenees dog, leaped up to join them. His huge body took up half the seats. "Mom and Dad will be home soon. Don't worry," Colin said, trying to reassure them both.

"Colin, look at the table. Every time the sky lights up, that candle from Poland seems to brighten." Even the dogs' attention was directed toward the candle. As both siblings stared at it for a minute, Elise whispered, "Grandma said the relative from Poland who gave it to us said to light it *only* if there was a lightning storm or somebody died."

"Was *going* to die, you mean."

Throwing off the blanket, Elise walked over to the table. "I think she called the candle a gromnica. Her cousin said it was like a magic candle with special powers."

"That's silly. Grandma said that's just some superstition that her Polish ancestors believed in."

As she touched the intricate carving on the golden candle, Elise asked, "Why is the security light aiming its beam right on the candle?"

"Hmm, as if it's drawing our attention to it."

Elise stood mesmerized by the lovely, unique gromnica. "I think we're supposed to light the candle right now, but I'm afraid of matches."

"I learned how to safely light a match at Indian Guides camp when I was in second grade. It's easy." Colin reached behind the pewter plate on the mantle to find the box of matches. "Mom and Dad won't get mad. That's what this candle is for." Setting the base of the candle on the floor, he flicked the blue tip of the match against the side strip and deftly lit the golden candle. With both dogs cuddled up next to them, they sat back on the couch. Elise placed her furry blue blanket around her shoulders.

Colin tried his cell phone again, this time calling his grandfather's phone. "This has never happened before on my phone. It shows a ninety-nine percent charge. So, I don't understand why I can't get through to anyone."

At the sound of a distant hum, Noah's ears perked up, and he stood frozen. "It sounds like planes in the sky, Colin!" Elise yelled as the rattle sound grew louder and transformed into a strange tearing, rasping noise. "Colin, look at that candle!"

The flame on the gromnica shot up almost to the ceiling while the sounds outside took on a more sinister and disturbing quality. "It sounds like giant flying insects!" Colin screamed, wrapping his little sister in his arms as the dogs nuzzled their way into the children's desperate embrace.

The noises stopped, and the flame sputtered and extinguished without warning. A few seconds later, an explosion rattled every wall and piece of furniture in the house. Instinctively, Colin covered the four of them with the blanket. Then…silence.

"I think the storm stopped," Colin said as he peered out from under the blanket. "Well, nothing fell down on us, so everything must be okay."

"Wait—where *are* we?" Elise asked.

"Look, there's smoke in the distance." Colin pointed as he felt dry, crinkly leaves below his knees. "This isn't our family room or even our backyard. It's a forest!"

Elise gazed up at the bright blue sky and felt the dry ground. "Maybe we're in a dream—like *The Wizard of Oz*."

Too startled to disagree, Colin reassured their equally frightened dogs and looked around. "It's hot outside. Like summertime."

The children started walking in the direction of the smoke, and after a short distance, they came across a small farm with a cow and chickens. Joining hands, they ambled past the barn. "Colin, look over there! A little cabin. Maybe they can help us."

"I guess there's no point in worrying about strangers." Colin pulled up his socks and brushed the grass from his knees. "Good thing we have Noah in case they aren't friendly. He scares everyone."

Staying close to her brother's side, Elise caressed the blanket as they walked toward the gate. "Wow! This is a really old place. Maybe it's abandoned."

"We'll ask to use their cell phone to call the police."

"Maybe they're too poor to have a cell phone," Elise replied as they continued toward the door.

"*Everybody* has a cell phone. Even homeless people have them," Colin chided, unable to resist rolling his eyes at his younger sister's ignorance. He then gently took her hand and squeezed it. "We'll find help and get out of here before it gets dark. Don't worry."

In the distance, they heard the rumble of a truck and saw not just one, but a string of trucks and jeeps approaching on the dusty road. "Get inside the gate!" Colin yelled, and they scurried through and quickly closed it. Crouching behind the rickety gray fence, they tried their best not to be detected, but Noah and Leia leaped into protective mode. Noah jumped onto the fence and started barking.

"Soldiers! Those are soldiers with guns, Colin!" Elise whispered as five vehicles flew past, throwing clouds of dust in the air.

"I guess those soldiers didn't see us. I can't believe they didn't care about the dogs."

The last truck in the convoy paused, went into reverse, and stopped next to the gate. A soldier jumped out and held his revolver in position to fire. After walking around the front of the house, he stood and shook his head. "Makes no sense. The gate flew open just before the first truck approached and then closed, but there's nobody here."

The driver leaned out of the truck and yelled. "Gerhard, it was probably just the wind."

Gerhard put his hand in the air. "There isn't any wind."

"Then it was a breeze from all the trucks passing by. It's nothing. Trust me!"

Gerhard shook his head in disbelief and appeared to glance in the direction where Colin and Elise were crouching by the fence. The dogs ran from one end of the fence to the other and continued their best attempts to frighten the soldier, but were ignored.

"Come on. We must get to the crash site before the partisans do. Get in!"

Gerhard clambered in, and the truck ripped down the road to catch up to the others.

Colin's jaw dropped, and his eyes opened wide as he turned to his sister. "Elise, this might sound really goofy, but I think those were German soldiers. Remember that little model of a missile Papa gave me from Poland? I think that's what just exploded!"

"Do you think the dust cloud and the roar we heard could have been a missile crash? Not a ten-inch model, but a *real* missile?" Elise asked excitedly.

"Grandma said the Germans launched those missiles right over her great-grandmother's house during the war."

"Colin…are we in Poland?"

Colin shook his head in disbelief. "Not only do I think we're in Poland, but I think we're right in the middle of the Second World War!"

Polish Wilderness in Niwiska's Forests

Chapter Two

The Polish Wilderness

The tattered wooden door to the old cabin creaked open, and an old woman with a long brown dress and printed apron appeared. She wore a reddish scarf on her head tied in the back. "Children, are you lost?"

Both dogs ran toward her and wagged their tails. Leia, as usual, jumped up to be stroked while Noah nuzzled close to gain his share of her attention. Colin and Elise ran to the dogs to pull them away.

"Hi, yeah, I guess we are lost," Colin said hesitantly.

"We are definitely lost and have no idea where we are." Elise tried hard to maintain her composure, but tears misted her aqua-colored frame glasses.

"Come inside where you'll be safe." The woman hurried the children into the house. "But no dogs, they stay in the yard." Elise's eyebrows furrowed, and her lips quivered. "Okay, only the little one can come in. The big one stays outside."

As Colin listened to the woman, he detected a faint hum that sounded like another voice while she spoke. He studied her lips and noticed they didn't exactly match her words. A faint voice uttering a foreign language was in the background, but English words were coming out of her mouth.

"Sit here on the bench, children. I need to fetch my daughter and grandson." The woman moved briskly through the back door, and Colin and Elise were left alone.

The fragrance of lavender wafted through the small home. "Colin, this is just how Grandma described the house her grandfather used to live in. A dirt floor and a big oven with pots and bowls over there."

"It smells pretty good in here." Colin gazed at the bunches of herbs and plants hanging from the rafters. "She seems like a nice old lady, but this is all too weird. We need to get out of here."

Elise whispered in her brother's ear. "Maybe we're like Hansel and Gretel, and she's a witch."

Both children overheard chatter of several people as the back door creaked open. "These children are dressed in the strangest way like I've never seen before. And the Germans didn't seem to notice them in our yard even though they were in plain view!"

A cheery-faced woman, who appeared to be about their mother's age, ran toward Colin and Elise. "Children, you must be hungry. I'll get you something to eat."

Standing at the door was a stone-faced boy who just stared at the two. He had acorn-colored hair and was close to Colin's age. "What village did you come from? Where are your parents?"

"Adam, the children must be frightened. I'm Maria, and this is my mother, Jadwiga and my son, Adam." The kind lady smiled. "And what are your names?"

"I'm Colin, and this is Elise, my sister. We're from Ohio."

"Ohio, that's not in Poland," Maria replied. "But Ohio sounds familiar."

"Ohio! That's where Michael and Marya live!" Jadwiga sprang to her feet, and her eyes lit up. "You must be their children. I dreamed you were coming, but I expected one of my grandsons. They're American soldiers!"

"No, our parents' names are Jessica and Greg Anderson, and we weren't ever planning on coming here." Elise teared up as she thought about her parents.

Adam moved closer to inspect Colin and then bent down to touch his shoes. "Those are the strangest boots I've ever seen." With a somber expression, he asked, "Why aren't you in bare feet? It's summertime."

"It was pretty cold when I left Ohio, so I had on my shoes. Anyway, these aren't boots. They're athletic shoes."

Adam noticed what Colin was wearing. "Why are you in your underwear, or are those the pants of a little boy?"

Elise glared at Adam. "Just so you know, all the boys where we come from wear shorts almost all year round. That's what the cool boys like my brother wear."

"So, when it snows, you wear shorts?" Adam remarked with a sarcastic tone.

"If it's warm enough, yeah," Colin retorted.

"All men should wear long pants," Adam said to Colin. "How old *are* you?"

"Thirteen," Colin responded. "Elise is ten. How old are *you*?"

"The same. You're thirteen? You look older."

"Adam, these children are lost. No more questions!" Maria rapped her son on the side of his head. "Where's your hospitality?"

Elise's eyes grew wide. She had never been hit or spanked in her entire life, nor had she ever seen an adult slap a child.

"I apologize for Adam's rudeness, but we're all mystified by your clothing." Maria moved closer to inspect Elise's top and pants. "So much color and pictures on them!" She touched the fabric and tugged at it. "It stretches and is so silky. And your glasses are so beautiful. Not like our wire-rimmed ones. I've never seen clothes like these before."

"Children, it is an even greater mystery that a German soldier didn't take any notice of you or those dogs, especially the giant one," Jadwiga declared.

"That's Noah," Elise stated. "He's a really nice dog, but he barks a lot and scares people."

"Surely, that soldier would have stopped to question you. It's inconceivable that a German would just walk by two strangers with dogs, especially dressed the way you are." Jadwiga put her hands to her cheeks and shook her head.

"They would have put you two under arrest and shot your dogs." Adam's face seemed to show little sympathy.

"Shoot Noah and Leia? They wouldn't do that!" Elise yelled and began to tear up again.

Maria put her arms around Elise and sat next to her on the worn wooden bench. "Adam speaks the truth, child. The Nazis are monsters, and they would surely do just as Adam said. You need to be very careful."

Jadwiga squinted as she spoke. "But why didn't the soldiers see the children when even *I* could see them with these poor old eyes? Several trucks of soldiers drove right past with them in plain view, and only one truck stopped. That soldier saw the gate open and close but didn't see the children go through? That can't be!"

Maria put some bread and jam in front of Elise and Colin. "Let's get back to where you are from. You said, 'Ohio.' My brother and his wife live there, but you say Michael and Marya Bryk from Cleveland aren't your parents, and you don't even know of them?"

Colin shook his head, "Nope, never heard of them, and I don't know any people from Cleveland. I once went there for a hockey tournament, though!"

Elise's eyes lit up, "Colin, I think we *do* know about those people. Those are the names on one of Grandma's books about her grandparents, Michael and Mary, but they're dead."

"Dead? My son is dead, and no one told me?" Jadwiga shouted.

Colin shook his head and waved his hands to explain. "They've been dead a long, long time. Even my mom didn't get to meet them!"

"When was your mother born, Colin?" Maria asked.

Colin muttered to himself as he tried to calculate the year of his mother's birth. "Maybe sometime in the 1980s?"

"That can't be. It's only 1944," Adam uttered.

Colin sat for a few moments in silence. "I need some paper to figure this out, but is that World War II going on out there?"

"Of course, it is! The war's been going on for five years now!" Adam walked over to a chest and opened the heavy lid. "I'll get you one piece, but we've only a few sheets left, so don't waste it."

Jadwiga put her finger to her lips, and her eyes stared at the peculiar dark painting above the fireplace. "Children, The Great War happened about twenty-five years ago, and now another war is going on in the world, so, yes, it's World War II."

"This has to be a crazy dream for all of us, but I'm not waking up from it." Maria stared at both children in puzzlement. "Could it be these children are from the future? Not even the rich people around here dress like this."

"There's another explanation. These children could be a miracle sent from God above." Jadwiga bobbed her head. "Yes, that's the only explanation."

Jadwiga Bryk in front of her home in Niwiska, Poland.

Chapter Three

Jozef meets the children

Noah's low but powerful bark preceded the sound of clumping boots on the back porch. Everyone startled, including Jadwiga. "Maybe it's Jozef returning home from work."

The door swung open, and a man smelling of the forest walked casually into the house. He stopped at a little bowl nailed to the wall, dipped his hands in to wet them, and proceeded to tap parts of his forehead. Elise and Colin sat frozen at the table, and then Elise ran to scoop Leia into her arms.

"This time the Germans got there before we were able to," said the bearded man, scowling. He walked right past the two children sitting at the table. "Jozef's in the barn and asked if I would bring him a cup of coffee."

The man held out two beaten-up metal cups for Jadwiga to fill from the large pot on the stove. He stood waiting at the head of the table and looked at Maria and Adam as he spoke. "Adam, pretty soon you'll be old enough to join us in the forests. No more little boy, right?"

Adam looked him squarely in the eyes, "Skory, I know how to handle a gun as well as any of you partisans, but Uncle Jozef wants me here to watch the house while Mama and Babcia are at work at the manor house."

"Friends, the Germans have taken everything of value from our homes. Why should anyone stay around to protect them? Adam needs to be a man serving his country. He's not a little boy anymore."

Jadwiga and Maria just nodded but carefully studied the eyes of Jozef's fellow forester, Skory. Colin and Elise didn't move a muscle; they wondered why this man didn't take notice of them or the dogs. Surely, he should have asked about the new guard dog barking at him in the yard.

"Well, off I go. Peace be with you." Skory held onto the coffee mugs but spilled a few drops onto the ground. He exited out the back to walk to the barn, and no one said a word until he was gone.

"Skory didn't take the slightest notice of the children or the barking dog," Maria remarked.

Jadwiga sat mystified. "Why is it that we can see and hear the children and that dog, but the Germans and Skory couldn't? The only logical answer is that this is a miracle."

Colin took out a pencil from his pocket and began to make a chart. "Okay, I'm going to draw one of those charts Grandma uses in genealogy to write out her family tree. She says to start with yourself, so these squares are Elise and me, here's Mom and Dad, and here's Grandma and Papa. We need to follow this line through Grandma's mom and dad."

"Put Stanley in that square," Elise instructed. "That was Grandma's father's name."

"Colin, can I look at that thing you are using to write? Is this thing from the future you live in?" Adam asked.

"I guess so. It's just a pencil. I have lots of them back home."

Jadwiga interrupted. "Wait! You said his name was Stanley? That's the name Michael put on the back of his son Stanley's picture. Let me get it to show you!"

Jadwiga ran to the same chest where she kept all their precious papers and returned with black and white photos. "Here, Michael's son Stanley is a very well-educated man. Here's his picture from when he graduated from high school."

Colin pointed to the photo. "I think that's the same man who's in that photo frame at Grandma's house. Grandma put all the medals he won during the war in it with his picture."

"We have lots of his pictures in the photo album Grandma made about her family. I'm sure that's him!" Elise exclaimed.

"Stanley's real name was Stanislaus. He's the youngest son of Michael, our eldest son." Jadwiga clasped her hands and again claimed that a miracle had just happened. "Colin, make another square here and then put in Michael's name and one more at the top and put in Jadwiga and Jan."

"Who's Jan?" Colin asked.

"That's Jadwiga's husband, but he died about twenty-five years ago," Maria said.

"I remember Grandma telling us about that!" Elise put her hands to her lips and lowered her head. "I'm sorry he died."

"That's okay." Jadwiga gave Elise a sweet smile. "Yes, he's dead, but no more talk of death. I have so many more questions to ask you."

"Let's look at this chart." Maria traced the boxes down to Colin and Elise's name. "So, I am your great-great-great-aunt, and Jadwiga is your great-great-great-grandmother!"

Everyone clapped their hands, and then Maria placed bowls in front of Colin and Elise. "First, let's get these children fed. I baked bread just this morning, and we have some soup on the stove."

Colin clapped his hands, but Elise crinkled her nose. "I don't eat soup."

"Elise! They probably make soup like Grandma makes. I LOVE Grandma's soup!"

"I'll eat some bread, though. Do you have any chicken nuggets?" Elise asked.

Colin groaned and whispered in Elise's ear. "You're going to eat what they give you, Little Missy. Do you see they don't even have a refrigerator in here? They wouldn't have chicken nuggets."

Maria laughed. "Everyone in Poland eats soup and bread, Elise. That's about all we have. We kill a chicken maybe only twice a year, so we have no chicken-whatever-you-call-them. I'm sorry."

Elise blushed over her ignorance. "I apologize. I have no idea what kinds of foods you eat."

Adam sat across from Elise. "I'll teach you what you need to know. We eat bread and marmalade, potatoes, cabbage, beets, and soup. Lots and lots of soup. Soup for breakfast and soup for lunch and dinner. Soup!"

Elise rested her chin on the palm of her hands. Back home, the only time she would even try one spoonful of soup was to get a dessert later in the meal—always at Grandma's insistence. Living during World War II was going to be even harder than she thought. Missiles, guns, Nazis, and now…soup.

Chapter Four

Meeting Jozef

"Adam, go to the barn and try to hurry Uncle Jozef into the house to meet Colin and Elise."

"Can I get a bowl for the dogs to have some water?" Adam asked.

Jadwiga nodded. "That's so thoughtful. I forgot all about the little one here." She reached down to pet Leia on the head. "I suppose I'll let you stay in the house. You can sleep on a mat, but the big one has to sleep on the porch."

"He'll make a good guard dog if we're the only ones who can hear him," Adam said. "I wonder if other animals can hear his barking?" Adam reached down to allow Leia to lick his hands. "This dog has no tail. Don't dogs in the future have tails?"

"Of course, look at Noah out there. He has a big long one that knocks things down. You don't want to get hit by his tail!" Colin laughed.

Adam smiled at Colin as he left through the back door.

Jadwiga was beaming. "I'm starting to get used to the idea of you being my great-great-great-grandchildren. What old person has ever met any of their family from this far back?"

Elise grinned and began to wander through the small house with just two rooms. "This is so different. It's like going to a log cabin in an old village in America."

Maria could see the confusion in Elise's eyes. "I sense our house is unlike any you have ever seen."

Elise's mind was ablaze as she considered how to answer the question without sounding rude or prideful. "Some people in America have tiny houses like this, but I don't see a bathroom anywhere, and well, I need to use one."

"It's outside, dear," Maria said. "I'll walk you out there."

"You mean, you use an *outhouse*?" Elise couldn't contain her surprise but was finally settling in on the idea that she would have to do lots of things that were repulsive to her. "I used one on a camping trip once. It didn't smell very nice."

"That's why it's set back from our house, Elise." Maria tried not to laugh. "Only very wealthy people have a toilet inside their home. This is a village of mostly poor farmers. At least, it *was* a village before the Nazis burned down their homes. Most of our neighbors had to move away from here."

"Why is that?" Elise asked.

"The Germans forced almost everyone out of their homes so they could build Camp Heidelager to train their soldiers. All around us are buildings, barracks, and training grounds the Germans use."

"I don't want to be rude or nosy, but why didn't *you* get kicked out?" Elise inquired.

"It isn't rude, dear. The truth is we had no relatives to go to because all of Mother's aunts and uncles were sent away a year before we received orders to leave. Mother and I agreed to work as cooks, and Jozef works as a forester. Everyone in Poland must work for the Germans. Everyone."

"So, you work as a cook at a restaurant?" Elise asked.

"Oh, heavens, no!" said Jadwiga. We work at the Hupka Manor House. It used to belong to Lord Hupka, but the Germans made him leave his own home. The German officers took over his beautiful home as their headquarters. That's where we go to work each day. Before the war, I was the priest's cook."

Maria motioned for Colin and Elise to look out the window. "Do you see that big white church over there across the road? That's our church, but the Germans closed it down, and it sits empty."

From the window, Maria saw Jozef running towards the house as Adam pulled him along. "Looks like Adam has already informed Uncle Jozef about you two. Let's go outside, Elise!"

"I still can't believe my eyes aren't playing tricks on me!" Jozef stopped just short of Elise and picked her up to spin her around. "You're as light as a feather! Don't they feed children in the future?"

Jozef set Elise back down on the ground. Shocked by his friendly welcome, Elise whirled a bit to catch her balance but smiled brightly. For the first time since they arrived, Elise was confident these were friendly and kind people who would look after her and Colin.

"So, what am I? Your great-great-great-uncle? Or do I add a few more greats?" Elise beamed at Jozef's warm and funny presence. He grabbed Elise's hand and kissed it while Elise giggled at this strange gesture. "You call me, 'Uncle Jozef.' Let's go inside so I can meet your big brother."

The sounds from the four boomed as they entered the house and Colin shot up in surprise. Jozef briskly walked over to Colin to shake hands. "I'm your Uncle Jozef, your grandma's great-uncle, as I understand." He kept shaking his head in disbelief. "I think my mother is right. This is a miracle!"

Elise ran over to Colin and whispered in his ear, "Uncle Jozef kissed my hand. I think he likes me better."

Jozef grinned. "Elise, here in Poland, all gentlemen kiss a lady's hand. That's what polite men do."

"Adam didn't kiss my hand," Elise remarked.

"We need to fix that now, don't we? Adam! Come here to kiss the lovely Elise's hand like a young Polish gentleman."

Adam lumbered over and went through the motions, but his effort certainly wasn't as gallant as Uncle Jozef's kiss. Elise curtsied, and everyone laughed and applauded their performance.

"Such a refined young lady is Elise!" Maria said. "Time for everyone to gather for dinner around the table."

Jadwiga had already set two loaves of hearty rye bread with something that looked like red jam in a bowl nearby. "Tonight, we have mushroom barley soup."

Jozef pulled out the chair for Elise. "Nobody cooks as well as my mother. She used to be the priest's cook until the Germans made him leave."

"Do you ever get to go to any church around here?" Colin asked.

Jozef shook his head. "Colin, we rarely go to church anymore because the church now sits empty. Not even a window or the bells remain."

"I helped Uncle Jozef bury the windows and the bells inside the forest where the Germans will never find them," Adam said.

"Why would you do that?" Elise asked.

"The Nazis would have melted down the bells for ammunition, and the bomb blasts would have shattered the windows," Jozef explained.

Jadwiga ladled the soup into wooden bowls and set them in front of everyone. "Father Kurek comes to visit and to give us communion when he can, but we have to say our prayers at home. God understands."

Elise stared at the strange foods inside her bowl as she swirled them around, hoping to avoid anyone noticing that she didn't want to try the soup. She hesitantly put a small spoonful of the soup in her mouth. All of a sudden, her eyes lit up. "This stuff is good!"

Jadwiga sliced off a large chunk of bread for everyone but gave Colin and Elise the largest portions.

"Tonight, we celebrate my American grandchildren's arrival."

"Babcia, I don't want to seem rude, but I bet they don't want to be here," Adam asserted.

Colin nodded his head in agreement. "Adam's right. We want to get back to America and even back to school. Can't believe I'm saying that. Elise and I have to figure out how to get back home. Right now, I have no idea how that's going to happen."

Chapter Five

The First Night in Niwiska

"Colin, you're going to sleep up in the rafters with Adam and Uncle Jozef, and Elise will snuggle up with Maria." Jadwiga fluffed up a pillow. "Here you are, my best down feather pillow for you."

"Can I sleep up in the rafters too? That sounds like fun." Elise showed her pearly white teeth and jumped up and down in anticipation of a fun sleepover with Colin and the guys.

"Tonight it's just the men up there. We ladies sleep down here." Maria motioned for Elise to sit on the bed. "Come here Elise, so I can brush your long, pretty curls."

Elise didn't mean for Maria to see the slight scowl on her face, but it was hard to hide her disappointment. Maria whispered, "Elise, I didn't want to say this in front of Colin, but little Leia would be more comfortable with you. That chubby little dog could never climb up ladders."

"You're right. Leia was supposed to be Colin's dog and mine, but she likes me best. I spend more time with her."

Jadwiga emerged from the other room in her nightclothes with her long gray hair cascading down her back. "Elise, Colin, come here so we can talk about tomorrow."

Colin ran over to the bed area and stared up at the strange, dark pictures above the beds. They seemed to be religious pictures from long ago. The people looked so sad and had their hands clasped together in prayer. He was grateful to sleep far away from this gloomy art.

"Tomorrow, Maria and I have to leave when the sun comes up to work at the manor house. I'll leave your breakfast on the stove. Adam will keep you company, but you must stay in the house. I still don't understand why some of us can see you and others can't, so we mustn't take any chances. Uncle Jozef will stop by during the day while he's making his rounds. Promise me you'll stay inside?"

Elise and Colin agreed as there were no other sensible options. "Yes, Jadwiga… or what do we call you?"

"I'm your Babcia now, just the same as for Adam." Jadwiga embraced each of them and rocked them back and forth. "Colin, say your prayers with Jozef and Adam. I imagine you are exhausted."

Clutching his pillow, Colin scurried up the ladder after Adam. Jozef wasn't far behind.

Colin removed his cell phone from his pocket and placed it on the wooden slats in front of him. "Might as well turn it off."

"What is that thing, Colin?" Jozef asked. "May I look at it?"

Jozef held the mysterious object up to a fading beam of the evening's light. "It looks like some of the components we find laying around the Germans' crash sites. What's it for?"

"You talk on it. It's a cell phone."

"A kid has a phone? Only our field agents have radio phones, and they're huge. Not like this tiny thing."

"Everybody has one of these where I live. We call each other and talk, text, and play games on it, but it wouldn't work here since you don't have cell towers. Sort of useless now."

"Colin, tell me more about your family—your mom and dad, and your grandparents."

Adam chimed in, "I want to hear about your house and school. You're so lucky to go to school!"

Colin's forehead wrinkled in disbelief. None of his friends considered themselves lucky to be in school. "Please don't think I'm bragging, but my house is bigger than this one. We have a kitchen, dining room, living room, four bedrooms, a basement, and three bathrooms."

Adam reclined on his side, "So your parents must be the rich people in your village like Lord Hupka used to be here in Niwiska?"

"Oh, no. Everyone in my neighborhood is like us, and some people have a lot more money than we do. A few of my friends even have pools in their backyard."

"Like pools of water to swim and fish in?" Adam asked.

"Sort of. We don't have one, but our neighbors in the back invite us over for pool parties."

"What a place this village you call a neighborhood must be! Rich people jumping in ponds to have fun!" Jozef laughed.

"Do you have horses and a carriage or a big car like Lord Hupka used to have?" Adam asked.

"My mom has a car, and my dad has a truck. Not the kind those Germans had, but still a truck."

Adam leaned forward with a confused look. "So, no horses?"

"No, we don't have a big enough yard for horses. I don't think we're allowed to have horses where we live."

"I suppose that's not so strange. My brother Michael, the one who lives in Cleveland, tells us he doesn't own a horse. Just walks to work or takes a big bus. Says his barn is only the size of a little toolshed." Jozef let out a giant chuckle.

Adam reclined on his stomach and held his head up with his fists. "Our house must be a big disappointment for you, Colin. Here, you have to sleep up in the rafters with the birds' nests."

Jozef tussled Colin's straight blond hair. "The same color hair, just like I used to have. That's not so strange since we are blood relatives, aren't we?"

"Uncle Jozef, maybe that's the secret. We can see Colin and Elise because they're our blood relatives. They still have some of our family's blood running through their bodies!" exclaimed Adam.

Jozef nodded his head in affirmation. "You might be onto something, Adam. None of the Germans saw them because they aren't related by blood, and Skory comes from a distant village and isn't family."

"So only people I'm related to can see me?" Colin asked. "Adam, you're pretty smart for a kid who doesn't go to school."

"Time for us to get some sleep, my young men. I must get up before the rooster crows. Just don't forget about chopping some of that wood, Adam. Babcia needs it for dinner."

Colin stared at the last soft glimmers of light that shone through the few cracks in the tightly-woven thatched roof. At first, he was certain no sleep would be his that night, but soon all his worries and thoughts melted away, and his mind retreated into wallowing blackness.

Chapter Six

What's a Partisan?

The next morning, Elise's eyes fluttered as she reached out for her blanket. She closed them for just a second before realizing she wasn't back home in Westerville. Maria stood at a basin washing her face and then fashioned her long, silky black hair into a bun on the back of her head.

"Maria, can I please come with you? I promise to be quiet and not cause any noise or trouble."

"Oh, my darling, I would love nothing better than to have you with me all day, but Mama and I work in a house with some ruthless and cruel men. What if all of a sudden, you become visible to them?"

Elise shook her head to show she understood and then smiled. Maria reminded her so much of her own mother back home. Her hair was long just like Elise's mother's but wasn't the same golden blonde. Having Maria around made her feel safe and protected. Last night, she even prayed with her in bed and sang songs to her, just like back home. While Elise thought Maria came close, nobody could replace the sacred bedtime rituals of her mother.

Uncle Jozef and the boys descended the ladder, and Elise sprung up to greet them.

"How did my little niece sleep last night?" Jozef inquired.

"Very well! I worried I might cry, but having Maria beside me made me feel like I was with my mom."

Jozef signaled for Elise to join him at the massive wooden chest. "I have something to keep you company while we are away." He pulled out a cloth bundle and unfurled the wrappings to reveal a doll, handmade of white cloth and slightly worn. It had an ornate black vest decorated with jewels and a colorful red skirt, similar to the one on the doll her Grandma had given her just days before.

"She's beautiful, just like my Polish doll at home!" Elise exclaimed.

"This dolly was my Valerie's." Jozef placed the doll in Elise's arms. "My little girl died two years ago."

Elise's eyes lit up, unsure if she should accept this gift. "I don't think it would be right for me to play with it."

"It is my honor to give it to you." Jozef stroked Elise's hair. "My little Valerie loved this doll, and it would bring me joy to see her loved again by one of my own."

Elise's eyes misted at the kindness of her newly-discovered uncle, but she now had so many questions. *How did his little girl die? Was Jozef once married? Was his wife killed in the war?*

"Did this doll have a name?" Elise asked.

"Valerie named her Eva after one of our cousins. Maybe you'll meet her."

Jadwiga emerged from the backdoor and beamed when she saw Elise caressing the doll while sitting next to Jozef. "Oh, Elise has Eva to keep her company. I made that doll, you know, every last stitch. Probably the most beautiful doll in the village, if I do say so myself!"

Jozef picked up the lunch pail his sister had just prepared for him. "Time for us all to leave, you three." He hugged the boys and kissed Elise on the forehead. "That doll has missed a little girl's love. Give her lots of attention today. Promise, Elise?"

Elise ran up to give Jozef another hug, "Thank you. Thank you so much for Eva! She'll keep me from crying." Elise considered herself a bit too old to play with dolls, but things were different here in Poland. She loved having this doll to help her through the day.

The adults waved their goodbyes and left the house through the front door. Adam walked to the cupboard and brought out three bowls. "Time for our morning meal. Come over to the oven to get yours."

"Cereal?" Colin asked.

"Zurek. We eat the same thing every morning." Adam began to demonstrate. "Like this, you put your cut-up bread in the bowl, and then I'll cut up this one boiled egg to share with you." Adam poured a sour-smelling broth over it. "Now, I'll cut up some horseradish to put on top. Babcia picked it fresh out of the garden, just this morning."

Both Colin and Elise's faces must have appeared to turn a little green, but they knew their breakfast would be this soup called Zurek—or nothing. The family's situation seemed quite desperate, and it wouldn't be kind of them to complain. Colin stirred his soup to cool it down. "This is so different than the foods we're used to."

Adam lifted his eyebrows. "No offense, but you two seem sort of spoiled, like you get everything you want."

Elise just shrugged, not sure if Adam was accurate in his judgment or if he was perhaps a bit jealous. "We have hungry people in our country too, but poor kids get fed at school for free. They get a free breakfast and lunch at school."

Adam's attention was only on his food as he noisily slurped his soup. "Must be nice to live in America. I got to go to school for a few years, but now I'm too old."

"So, you can read and write?" Elise asked.

"Of course, but mostly because of Uncle Jozef's help. School for us ended when the Germans arrived. Now, students can only attend up to the third level, and then they only learn to read a little and count and add numbers. No more history or science. The Germans want to keep us stupid, so we are only capable of following their orders."

"Why don't you just organize a protest against those rules, Adam?" Elise asked.

"Oh, boy! You have a lot to learn." Adam slurped another spoonful and kept shaking his head in disbelief. "The Germans would shoot me in the head if I protested, or at the very least, I'd get sent to a work camp. During the first years of the war, the Germans would be waiting outside the church and grab most of the young people, put them in trucks, and send them to work on farms or factories in Germany. I was still too young, but now I'm the right age to be sent away like that."

"Are you worried that might happen to you?" Colin inquired.

"All the time, but Colonel Heiss likes Babcia cooking in his kitchens, and he lets me stay. That's the way it is with the Nazis. If you are useful to them, they leave you alone… if you don't cause trouble. If you do, off you go to Germany or to work on some nearby farm."

"Grandma tried to tell us things like this, but I thought she was making it up. She's a writer," Colin said.

"A writer about this war? I never thought that someday people would know what was going on in Poland." Adam stood up to get more broth for his soup. "The Germans like Uncle Jozef's work in their forests too, but they don't know what he's really up to."

"What's that?" Colin asked.

"Do you know what a partisan is?"

Colin shook his head no.

"Before the war began, England and France made a promise to come to Poland's rescue if Germany attacked, but they never did. They thought their countries could make peace with Hitler, but then he attacked France, and the French surrendered almost the same day. Germany invaded Poland from the west and then Russia came from the east. It's lousy sitting in between two evil countries."

"But what's a partisan?" Elise asked.

"Some people call them the AK, but all the Polish people who pledge to fight to the death for Poland's freedom are called partisans. It took our soldiers and young people a while to regroup and coordinate after Germany invaded, but they managed to organize themselves into an army. Uncle Jozef is a partisan, but no one outside our family is supposed to know."

"Uncle Jozef is like a soldier? But I didn't see a gun on him." Colin's face contorted with confusion.

"You must have heard that missile explosion yesterday. That was a doodlebug missile. Last year, the Germans started to test-fire them right across our backyard. They land in fields all around here and cause huge craters. Uncle Jozef and the other foresters try to rush to the place where the missiles fall to get to them first. Then, they carry the missile pieces to a place where other partisans carry them to the Americans and English."

"Are the Americans close by?" Elise asked with excitement in her voice.

"No, but the Americans are over in France now. The Polish partisans have developed a whole network of workers to get the missile parts out of the country. It's very important work because no one has ever seen these types of weapons before."

"You're talking about a rocket, like the one my grandparents gave me!" Colin exclaimed.

"They gave you a missile?"

"No, just a model of one. Papa said it was a model of a V-2," Colin said. "I think I have a picture of it on my cell phone to show you." Colin retrieved his phone and booted it up to the photo gallery. "Look, right here. I'm sitting between my grandparents holding it."

"That's just how Uncle Jozef said it looks standing up straight at the launch site." Adam marveled at how Colin was able to enlarge the photo to show him the missile's details. "Uncle Jozef needs to see this. He said the English and Americans know very little about this newer one. You call it a V-2?"

"Let's see if my cell phone can call my parents. Sort of doubt it, but it's worth a try." Colin tried his parents' numbers again, but the same error message appeared. "Nope. Let me see if I can access the internet."

Adam sat dumbfounded but amazed at this device from the future.

"Oh my gosh, I got the Google search page!" Colin's hands shook with exhilaration. "Uh, what should I ask about?"

"I don't know. Germany? Hitler? Doodlebugs?" Adam was bewildered at the very question Colin was asking.

"You said no one knows much about the V-2, so why don't you ask about that?" suggested Elise.

"Okay, V-2. Let's see." Both Adam and Elise kept putting their faces in front of the screen. "Guys, get back. I can't read this."

"Are you getting anything, Colin?" Elise asked.

"Oh my gosh! I can't believe this! The internet works here! There's a whole mess of sources: V-2, The Nazi rocket that launched the space age, V-2 missile military technology, V-2 Rocket.com, the A4/V-2 resources site…" Colin jumped up and down, shouting the names of the site names. "Let's try this one… the history, diagrams, descriptions. Uncle Jozef is going to love seeing this!"

Elise grimaced and clenched her teeth. "One problem, Colin, your battery is down to ninety-seven percent… now ninety-six percent. It might run down to nothing if we keep your cell phone turned on."

Colin's excitement suddenly dissipated. "You're right. Let's power off and wait until Uncle Jozef gets home. I sure hope it powers back up, and this wasn't just a fluke."

Chapter Seven

The Internet

Elise and Colin sat impatiently inside the stuffy house as Adam busied himself with outside chores. Each time he came inside, Colin asked if he could be of any help, but Adam always declined the offer.

Colin paced back and forth, stopping every few minutes to pet Leia. "Just staying here all day is driving me crazy. There's nothing to do, and I can't even read the books Adam has stored in the attic. They're all in Polish."

Elise pulled the curtain aside to check on the outside. "Poor Noah, all alone in the yard, and we can't go outside to pet him."

"Stupid dog barks every time a truck goes by." Colin looked out the window facing the garden. "I wish Adam would come inside for lunch. I haven't seen him for over an hour."

Suddenly, Noah began to bark with more urgency. Elise timidly looked out the window. "Two old guys with a horse and cart are at the gate. Adam's with them!" Elise looked frantically around. "Where should we hide?"

"Let's go up the ladder into the loft." Colin grabbed his sister's arm to help her up.

"Wait. Leia has to come."

"No, Elise, we don't have time. She's too heavy to carry." Both children scurried up the ladder and peered down into the kitchen through holes in the loft's floor.

Adam rushed in through the back door and yelled for his cousins. "Colin! Elise! Where are you?" He frantically looked under the beds and in the old wardrobe.

"Adam, we're up here. Who are those guys?" Colin called down.

"They're safe. I fetched them to meet you." Adam opened the front door to allow the two men to come inside.

Although both were elderly, the man with the brusk wintery mustache seemed much stronger and held onto the other who appeared quite feeble. "Lord Hupka, sit here. I'll be right back with your jacket." He returned quickly and handed the coat to Adam. "Just in case the Germans come by, we'll tell them we brought a coat to Maria for mending."

"Come down, you two!" Adam furiously signaled for Colin and Elise to descend the ladder while Leia eagerly jumped on the men's pant legs. The younger man pointed at Leia using a firm voice. "Down!" Immediately, Leia rolled onto her back in a submissive posture. "This dog needs some discipline."

"Wow, that's just how Grandma controls Leia!" Elise whispered as she hid behind her brother.

"Now, where are these two Americans from the future?" asked the older man with the cane.

Adam put his arm around Colin. "Lord Hupka, Uncle Andrzej, this is Colin and Elise from America."

The younger man's eyes lit up. "Remarkable! I'm Andrzej, one of your great-grandfathers, Marya's papa. Adam showed me the diagram of our family that you made to explain all of this." Colin reached out and shook his hand, and then Elise emerged from behind her brother. She smiled sweetly with her doll in tow.

Lord Hupka adjusted his wire-framed eyeglasses. "I can't see a thing, but these must be the people from the visions I've had for the past five years." He grinned. "Can they hear me? I don't hear any voices."

Colin nodded. "Yes, I can see and hear Lord Hupka, but he obviously can't see or hear me."

"Somewhere in front of me must be the sweet Elise," said Lord Hupka. "Adam tells me Jozef gave her Valerie's precious doll. Jozef must be really taken by this Elise."

Elise frowned at the thought that Jozef's gift might have been too generous.

Adam put his arm around Elise to bring her to the two elderly men. Andrzej kissed her hand, and she sweetly curtsied. He then reached out for Elise to come closer so he could examine her face. "I see a bit of my Marya in your blue eyes and your delicate mouth. Marya was my oldest child. She would have been your great-great-grandmother."

Both men sat in amazement. "I'm so happy Elise has that doll," Lord Hupka said. "I am like Jozef. I never had children of my own. Everyone in the village is like my own family."

"I don't understand. Didn't Jozef have a wife—you know, Valerie's mother?" Elise asked.

Andrzej signaled for Elise and Colin to sit at his side on the bench. "No. At the beginning of the war, Jadwiga found a baby lying next to her mother's dead body in the woods. Jozef adopted the baby and told everyone, including the Germans, that Valerie's mother was his wife but had died. Valerie was a Jewish baby."

Elise stood speechless, and shivers ran down her spine. The story explained not only the mystery of Valerie's mother but the overwhelming kindness of Jozef.

"Jozef was the best father any little girl could have hoped for. He visits her grave every day on the way to work." Andrzej leaned back and crossed his arms. "Elise and Colin, realize now you are both a blessing to Jozef. He loves children."

Andrzej turned his attention to Colin. "My great-grandson Colin doesn't appear to be a child anymore. He's almost as tall as me!" Andrzej motioned for Colin to stand next to him and then chuckled. "Just a few more years, Colin. You'll be as tall as me." He then took on a more serious demeanor. "Let me tell you why we came to meet you, Colin and Elise. Lord Hupka and I want to know what happened before you arrived in Niwiska. What was it that brought you here?"

Colin brushed his fingers through his thick hair. "Elise and I were home by ourselves when a bunch of lightning appeared in the sky. All of our lights went off, but this candle that Grandma and Papa brought back from Poland seemed to have its own light source even though it wasn't lit."

Elise couldn't contain her excitement. "Then we remembered the instructions: we were only to light it in case of lightning or if someone was dying."

Colin continued. "Yeah, so we lit it and then it was like bombs were going off it our yard, and we covered ourselves with a blanket and ended up in your forest. Probably near those trees right over behind the barn."

"Remarkable, just remarkable!" Andrzej brought his hands into a prayer-like position. "What did this candle look like? The one you lit back at your house?"

"It was sort of old, but it was really fancy and all golden." Elise held up her hands to show how tall it was. "It had carvings in it of flowers and leaves, but when we lit it, the flames shot up to the ceiling!"

Andrzej carefully repeated what the children had just reported to Lord Hupka.

"Glory to God! That's my candle, the one I still have in my room!" Tears flowed from the old man's eyes. "I've had dreams and visions for the past five years that Americans were going to come to help us here in Niwiska. I had given up all hope for many months, but the dreams continued. I have the same dream every night. I thought the Americans would be soldiers sent to save us, not children with their dogs."

Everyone glanced at each other in disbelief.

"My parents received that candle on the day I was baptized in 1866. It's been sitting on the bureau in my bedroom every day of my life, and it's still there," Lord Hupka said. "How on earth did Colin and Elise's family all the way over in America get my candle from Poland?"

Colin scratched at his forehead. "Some relative of my grandma gave it to her last month when she visited Niwiska."

Lord Hupka stroked his beard while his weak eyes stared at a painting. "My father used to say that my gromnica was special and should only be lit to save a life. He also said it doesn't matter if the gromnica saves one life or many lives because every single life is precious."

Andrzej rose from his chair and squeezed Colin's shoulders. "I agree with your father, Lord Hupka. Colin and Elise didn't come from the future for no obvious reason. They were sent here during this horrible war to save lives."

Elise clutched Eva to her chest and trembled at the thought of fighting any Nazi. "But we're just kids! How are we supposed to help? I never even shot a gun before—ever!"

Andrzej formed his hands into a steeple. "Children, you were sent to this house on a mission that God has allowed. Like young David in the Bible, you are to use the gifts He gave you. David was good with a slingshot and killed the giant. Your gift is that none of the Germans can see you."

Adam had been listening intently and began to fidget. "Colin, maybe you should show Andrzej that special phone."

Colin pulled it out of his pocket and set it on the table. "I can't turn it on because the battery will start to drain, but maybe I can tell the partisans all about the missiles the Germans are firing over the village. Scientists must have been researching them since the war ended, and the internet has almost everything on it."

"You know when the war will end? Tell us, please!" Andrzej bellowed.

"I don't remember because we haven't studied much about the Second World War yet in school," Colin said. "I'll find out when I turn the phone back on. When Jozef returns."

Andrzej stroked his mustache as he studied Colin's cell phone. "Keep a close eye on that phone of yours. Niwiska has a few scoundrels who might try to steal that phone and sell it to the Germans for a pretty penny. Be cautious, Colin. Very cautious."

Chapter Eight

Amazing!

As soon as Jozef arrived from his job in the forest, Colin ran to tell him of Grandpa Andrzej and Lord Hupka's visit. "Lord Hupka has to be right. This journey into the past didn't just happen to scare us or teach us a history lesson." Colin clutched his cell phone as he silently considered all the possibilities. "Uncle Jozef, I want to come with you into the forests."

"Sorry, Colin. I know you want to help, but you have no idea of what you're asking. It's too dangerous out there." Jozef moved about the house, unable to settle in one place. "You don't know the forests, the dangers…" his voice trailed off. "Who knows if a stray bullet could hit you or if a wild boar attacked? No, the more I think about it, the more dangers come to mind."

"I was sent here on some mission, and that certainly wasn't to sit inside the house all day with my little sister." Colin's voice and demeanor became more confident with each passing minute.

"You have no idea what I do as a forester. I'm not just recording the height of trees and checking for ones to be taken down. My job is different now with all of these missiles in the forest."

Jadwiga sat down next to her son. "Colin's correct. The children have been sent here for some special purpose, and they need to be told. They need to know what is really going on here and the risks."

Jozef buried his forehead in his hands and puffed out a deep breath. "Are you ready to hear what my men are doing in the forests? Elise needs to hear this too if it means her brother wants to risk his life. She also has to agree."

The two siblings looked at one another, and Elise bit her lip. "Grandma would tell us bedtime stories of our relatives who came to America and how they sacrificed and were so brave and courageous. She used to say, 'You inherited these ancestors' DNA, and their spirit is in every part of your body, in your blood, your hands, your feet, and in your heart.' I want to be brave like them, too."

Adam looked puzzled. "What's DNA?"

"That's something scientists say are in every single cell in our body from the time we were first created. We get it from our parents," Colin explained.

"What's a cell? Like an AK cell?" Adam asked.

Elise rolled her eyes at her cousin. "What I'm trying to say is that my brother is just as brave as anyone who has ever lived, and if he wants to help, I'm with him all the way."

"Even if he dies while he is trying to help? Have you thought this through carefully, Elise?" Maria asked.

Elise rested her head on her brother's arm. "There are things that you must do, no matter what."

Everyone, even Jozef and Adam, had tears in their eyes as they pondered the bravery of these two children.

"Alright, I'll tell you most everything, but some details must be kept a secret from you. I can only tell some things to my cell. Colin, Elise. While I work as a forester in the wilderness forests of Niwiska and Blizna, I'm also a member of the AK. I'm a Home Army partisan. I pledged my life to fight for the freedom of Poland. If the Germans find out I'm collecting missile fragments to send to England, or they discover I've sabotaged their railway to blow up the tracks, they would shoot me on the spot. No trial, no mercy. Instant death."

Jozef hesitated, worried that people from the future could never understand their dire situation, but continued. "Do you understand how serious this is? If I'm discovered and killed, everyone in this house would be arrested and sent to Pustkow, the concentration camp just up the road."

Both Colin and Elise's faces were dower. They hadn't considered that Adam, Maria, and even Jadwiga would also suffer the same fate as Jozef.

Jadwiga stood up from her chair and put her hands on the table and leaned over, facing the children. "Jozef, they also need to know that we three also consider ourselves partisans. I may not go into the forest with a grenade or a rifle, but Maria and I are the eyes and ears for the Home Army. Maria understands German and often listens in on their private conversations. I understand most, but the German officers don't know that and talk more freely when I'm around. They think I'm a stupid old lady who only speaks Polish."

Maria smiled as she saw Colin and Elise's eyes perk back up. "We go home and tell Jozef or anyone else we trust from the Home Army about what we overheard. I sometimes read the Germans' reports that Heiss leaves carelessly laying on his desk."

Jadwiga continued. "So you see, Maria and I also risk our lives. Adam helps by retrieving the secret Home Army newsletter your Grandpa Andrzej prints in his barn."

Adam beamed now that his secret was out. "I took the oath two years ago."

"We all did, at least in our hearts." Maria held her hand over her chest and then pointed her finger up to the heavens. "We made our pledge to God, and that is far more important than any made to man."

"Can I take the oath now? I'm ready." Colin stood up with his hand on his heart.

Jozef stood in front of Colin and smiled at his bravery. "For you, the oath will be a little different because you are an American. Repeat these words after me: *Before God Almighty, I pledge my help to fight for my ancestors' country, the Republic of Poland. I pledge to steadfastly guard her honor, and to fight for her liberation with all my strength, even to the extent of sacrificing my own life. I pledge unconditional obedience to the President of Poland, the Commander-in-Chief of the Republic of Poland, and the Home Army Commander whom he appointed. I pledge to resolutely keep secret whatever may happen to me. So help me, God!"*

While repeating the pledge, Colin held his shoulders back with his chest thrust out. In everyone's mind, he had grown six inches taller and had suddenly become a man.

Chapter Nine

Colin's Work Begins

"This isn't fair." Adam stood with his hands on his hips, his face a dark shade of red. "Colin's been here only a few days, and he gets to go with you to meet the partisans? I have to sit here all day babysitting Elise?"

"I can take care of myself without any of your help," Elise said. "Besides, I'm invisible, so just pretend you can't see me if you don't like it." Elise sassily bounced her head back and forth while she placed the cleaned bowls in the cupboard.

"Enough of your complaining, Adam." Maria lifted the heavy kettle onto the ceramic stove and wiped her hands on her apron. "Elise, you've become such a big help to Jadwiga and me with cleaning and peeling the vegetables, as well as baking the bread."

"Too bad we can't bring you to the manor house. You work harder than any of the other girls who are twice your age. And you're a lot sweeter, too!" Jadwiga wrapped her arms around Elise and rocked her back and forth while they embraced.

"I could come. Please! No one would see me," Elise begged.

"Out of the question. I don't want the Germans to turn you into a slave laborer like everyone in the village has become," Jadwiga said. "Anyway, you're so very useful here."

Elise's mouth turned downward, and Maria noticed her niece's disappointment. "Don't be so sad. I know it must be so boring here for you, but you have a purpose. You may not realize this, but Jozef was incredibly sad and depressed before you arrived. You have helped bring our old Jozef back to life. Valerie's death was so painful. He almost lost the will to live."

"How did Valerie die?" Elise asked.

"It was a terrible time for us about two years ago." Jadwiga's face was downcast as she spoke. "That winter was brutal, and so many people came down with typhoid fever, and many died. Valerie lasted only about five days. She was so weak."

Maria added, "Now we all have you, Elise. You are pure joy and such a beautiful child inside and out. Having you here has kept all of our spirits high and given us a renewed determination to keep up our fight."

Elise smiled and hugged each woman. "How much longer do you think the war will last?"

"We've heard reports the Americans are pushing eastward in this direction." Jadwiga closed her eyes and smiled. "I dream of my grandson, Stanley, coming into the village to rescue us. He is driving a big American truck with your wonderful flag on the side."

"Wouldn't that be something if your own great-grandfather showed up in the village, and you could meet him?" Maria smiled and laughed at the thought.

Jadwiga bit her lip, and her eyes suddenly looked sorrowful. "The Russians are much closer to Niwiska, and they will likely be the ones to liberate us if the war ever ends."

Elise remembered her grandmother telling her that history had not been kind to Poland. It sat between two aggressive and evil empires who only wanted to devour it. She also remembered Grandma saying the Russians were just as bad as the Germans, but somehow Poland must have ended up just fine because her grandparents talked all the time about what a great place it was to visit. If only she had listened more carefully!

"I've finished the last sketches, but now my phone is down to sixty-three percent. I'm sorry, Uncle Jozef; I don't understand all this technical stuff in these reports." Colin sat at the table and put the final label on the diagram. "I hope the English and American scientists can figure out all of my descriptions."

Jozef held up two of Colin's drawings containing hundreds of details he managed to copy from the internet images. "Everyone in my unit and our commander can't stop talking about your work. They all call you "The Young Partisan.' You're quite the hero!"

"Adam's been helping me these past four days. He draws much better straight lines than I do and writes the words in Polish. Without his help, these diagrams would make no sense." Colin and Adam's eyes met, and the boys smiled at one another.

"I can hardly wait until the future to get one of those phones!" Adam exclaimed.

Colin nodded and then lowered his eyes to the table. He didn't want to tell his cousin that phones like this wouldn't come out for another seventy or so years.

"Are you ready to meet your unit, Colin?" Jozef tucked the loaves of bread and hunks of cheese into the two sacks. "I'll have to carry both until we meet up with Father Kurek."

Colin's eyes brightened. "I get to meet Father Kurek today?" Colin rushed to embrace everyone in the house, and the last was his little sister. "Don't spend any time worrying. Today's just a trip to meet my unit, so I'll be in no danger." He kissed Elise on the forehead and gave her a huge hug. "No tears or anything like that. Promise?"

Elise pursed her lips and tried not to tear up while her brother left through the back door with Uncle Jozef. She ambled over to Maria and curled up in her lap.

"It's okay to cry. You're still a little girl, and you love your big brother." Maria rocked Elise for just a bit and then remembered, "I forgot to tell you. Jozef said Father Kurek was coming home with him for dinner. You'll get to meet our priest. He truly is the kindest priest in all of Poland."

"I heard stories about him from Grandma. He worked as a partisan in the Home Army and got caught by the Germans."

"No, he didn't, Elise. You must have gotten him confused with another person. He only serves as their chaplain and says mass for them out in the forest. The Germans know he rides his bike all around the villages to say mass and give us communion. He even baptizes the babies after they're born. He manages to stay safe."

"Maybe I didn't listen all that carefully to the stories. They seemed like they took place so long ago, and neither of us understood much until we traveled back to the war. Grandma talked about so many people, and it was all like a big muddle in my mind." Elise enjoyed Maria's warm embrace but always thought of her momma when they cuddled. A wave of sadness came over her.

"I wonder how this is all going to end for us. You and Colin, Mama, Jozef, and my Adam. We're all so weary of being fearful and following the rules so no one will be punished or arrested. I've heard so many stories about how cruel the Nazis have been and then the horrible things I've seen with my own eyes. Too terrible to even repeat!"

Jadwiga strolled over to the table to join them. "Most of these Germans are like monsters. A few have their good moments, like Colonel Heiss. He likes my cooking, so he gives me a few extra foods from the kitchen to supplement our meals at home. It costs him nothing, and I keep his belly full. If I fell and broke a leg, he would surely treat me like any other old woman."

Elise kindly studied Jadwiga's thin body. Jadwiga was about her grandmother's age but seemed much older. She had just as much energy as Grandma, but Elise knew her life was much more difficult in Poland. Jadwiga and Maria had to walk at least a mile back and forth to the manor house each day. Adam had told Elise the best place to sleep during winter was on top of the huge ceramic oven top, so Jadwiga probably felt cold all winter long. Elise marveled that Jadwiga could carry two heavy sacks of potatoes at one time and rarely sat down to rest. Everyone in Niwiska worked so hard.

"Maria, I wish I could say I wasn't worried about Colin—and Jozef too—but I am. Would you tell me some of those old fairytales like from the night before last? Maybe that will help. Please?"

"Let me tell you about Jurata, the Queen of the Baltics.

Ages and ages ago, on the bottom of the Baltic Sea, there was a splendid palace belonging to Jurata, the Queen of the Baltic waters.

Not only was the queen beautiful, but thrifty as well. She ruled her kingdom justly and cared for the welfare of her subjects. Even when her favorite fish, the flounder fish, was served, the kind-hearted queen ate only half of each fish and threw the other half back into the sea.

Imagine, if you can, the queen's indignation when she learned that a fisherman who was a stranger in her kingdom was seen casting his net at the mouth of a river. The queen decided to entice the fisherman into her amber boat and then punish him for violating her laws. But, when Queen Jurata saw the handsome young fisherman, she declared her love to him.

Every evening, she swam to the shore to meet her sweetheart. However, jealous Piórun, the god of thunder, became angry and threw down thunderbolts and destroyed the queen's sea palace, killing the queen and her courtiers. Piórun chained the fisherman to the sea bottom. To this day, when there is a storm, you can hear his laments. The amber jewels which are cast ashore by the waves of the Baltic are fragments of Jurata's amber palace."

Elise winced. "I don't think that story made me feel any better. I like the one about the cat and pussy willow much better."

Maria embraced Elise even tighter. "I'm sorry. It seems most of the fairytales I know don't end with much happiness. Sort of like the way our lives are right now with the war raging."

Chapter Ten

Colin Meets His Unit

The morning light cast its shadowy beams onto their path as they meandered through the dense pine forest. Colin followed behind Jozef, stepping carefully to avoid the thick tree roots intertwined with the delicate plants. Jozef stopped every few minutes to survey their surroundings.

"Let's stop here for a rest and go over all of the basics again." Jozef removed the pack that would be Colin's.

"I can carry that backpack, Uncle Jozef."

"I'm not sure if strangers will see just a sack floating in the air or if it becomes invisible on you. We'll find out when we arrive."

Colin chuckled. "That would be weird."

"I've told the men in my unit about you, even the ones who aren't your blood. They are like our brothers, so you'll be in no danger."

"I'm not going to run into any German soldiers, right?"

"Unlikely. And remember: they can't see you. I'm giving you this gun on the off-chance that something happens to me." Jozef snapped open the flap that secured the sack and pulled out a revolver.

Colin reached out to touch it. "I've never EVER even fired a gun."

Jozef stood with his feet apart and aimed at a tree. "Hold it steady like this with both hands, aim, and pull the trigger."

Colin's eyes lit up at the thought that he might have to kill another human being, but recalled the solemn oath he gave. He took the revolver from Jozef and modeled the correct stance.

"Just like that. You have a strong upper body, so use every muscle to keep steady." Jozef reached out for the gun and returned it to the sack.

"This forest goes on forever." All Colin could see were trees and birds flitting from branch to branch. Only the rustle of an occasional squirrel scurrying through the dried leaves surprised Colin.

"This forest is both our protector and provider, but it now shares the same destiny as the villagers. We're both controlled and manipulated by the Germans. Each tree is like a person; we might be cut down if it benefits the Reich." Jozef shrugged. "A tree or a person—our fate is the same."

"What do these yellow and red stripes on some of the trees mean?" Colin asked.

Jozef chuckled. "To a forester, the different colors and stripes indicate which trees should be cut down in the next year. The Germans don't know that the yellow stripes guide our path so we don't get lost. Look at the back of this tree. Do you see the yellow stripe with a red dot?"

Colin went behind the tree to check out what Jozef was referring to.

"That tells us to follow this path to our encampment. We move all the time to keep the Germans off our trail."

"So, even partisans can get lost in the forest?"

"For those of us who grew up in this wilderness area, that is unlikely. But now these forests are swarming with partisans from all over Poland because of the German missile launches. We collect intelligence and missile fragments for the Allies."

"So, the Allies are the Americans?"

"The English, also. I suppose you can say the Russians are our allies, but the Poles don't trust any of them. We Polish people only want to regain our freedom."

After an hour's trek, Colin and Jozef noticed the smoky air not too far ahead. "Not much farther, Colin!"

Colin was relieved his long journey was coming to an end; his legs were beginning to feel like rubber. As they approached, the group of about a dozen partisans froze like statues until they recognized Jozef.

The first to approach was a bespectacled man with a white collar and long black gown. His gaze circled Colin's frame, and he pulled his glasses closer to his eyes. "Jozef, is this the young man from America?"

"Colin, this is Father Kurek, our chaplain and fellow partisan," Jozef said. "He can see you because he's a distant cousin of mine."

"My word! Everything Jozef reported is absolutely true!"

Colin reached out his hand to shake the priest's. "Hello," was all Colin was able to muster. "I don't think I've ever met a real priest before."

"Don't they have priests in the future?" Father Kurek's brows wrinkled.

At that moment, the other partisans who could see Colin ran up to greet him, shaking his hand and slapping him on the back. Colin's face radiated from the unit's welcome and comradery. He immediately felt like he belonged.

One man, who was dwarfed by all the others, took Colin by the arm and brought him to their gathering place around the fire. "Do you want some coffee, young man?" Colin was parched, so he reached out for the tin mug and took a sip. His grimace and wrinkled nose caused an explosion of laughter from the group. "Sorry. It's not real coffee. We make this stuff from roasted acorns. The Germans call it ersatz coffee. Don't feel bad. We all think it's awful!"

Jozef introduced each man to Colin and explained their blood relationship, but Colin's mind was overloaded. He was now a celebrity and an expert, and a magician and historian, all rolled into one person.

After explaining the Columbus Blue Jacket's logo on his jacket and why he wore short pants, Colin had a few questions of his own. "How do you guys all live out here in the forests? Do you ever get to go home?"

One, who appeared to be just a few years older than Colin, was the first to tell his story. "I'm your cousin Peter. About six months after the invasion, the Germans picked up about twenty of us younger people to work on a big collective farm run by a German. I ran away and found my way into the forests in hopes of joining up. I spent three weeks wandering, stealing from the villagers' barns to survive. It was winter, and I was sure that death was at my door, but then two partisans found me, and I joined up with their cell."

Colin's jaw dropped at the danger this young cousin had experienced. "One thing I don't understand. Sometimes you say 'cell' and other times 'unit' when you talk about yourselves. What's the difference?"

A clean-shaven man with brown wavy hair and wearing an impressive greenish-gray uniform came to sit next to Colin. "A cell is maybe three or four men, and a unit has several cells within it. Here you see most of our unit, and we all report to headquarters in Kolbuszowa."

"Colin, shake hands with our captain, Jozef Batory. You'll not meet a finer officer in the Home Army than this man."

"I have no idea of how we are related, Colin, but it must be so since I can plainly see you. My family is from this area, so it's possible. Many of us are probably cousins, but the stories and connections have been lost over the years," Captain Batory said.

Colin was dazzled by the brilliant blue designs on the collar of his uniform, which also had many silver buttons on the shoulders and down the front.

"Captain Batory does not often travel to our posts, but he wanted to meet you personally and see that cell phone of yours," Jozef said.

Colin quickly pulled the phone out of his pocket. "Sorry, but I don't turn it on unless I need to. There's a battery inside that powers it, and I don't want to waste the charge. That is, unless you have a special question."

Jozef pulled out Colin's sketches and descriptions of the missiles. "Look here, Captain. Colin has made detailed drawings of the inside of the rocket and wrote out descriptions of how it works."

"Remarkable! Just remarkable!" Captain Batory sat back down on the log and spent several minutes scanning the papers. "This information explains so much, like the composition of the fuel, how to wire the control gear and guidance systems. The entire missile has been a mystery, up until now. Remarkable!"

Colin's face turned red, but he was pleased his hard work was deemed important by this esteemed officer.

"Colin, you need to stand proudly. I'm declaring you to be an official member of the Home Army. Your uncle told me you already took your oath." Captain Batory pulled out a pin and a cloth band from his top pocket. "Not only that—I'm making you an honorary first lieutenant in the Armia Krajowa."

Colin's eyes bugged out, and he stood at attention as Captain Batory placed the pin on his shirt. "You realize you now outrank everyone here except me, right?"

Uncle Jozef leaned over to shake his nephew's hand. "Don't let this go to your head. Remember, you don't know your way out of this forest!"

Everyone howled and ran up to shake Colin's hand and salute him.

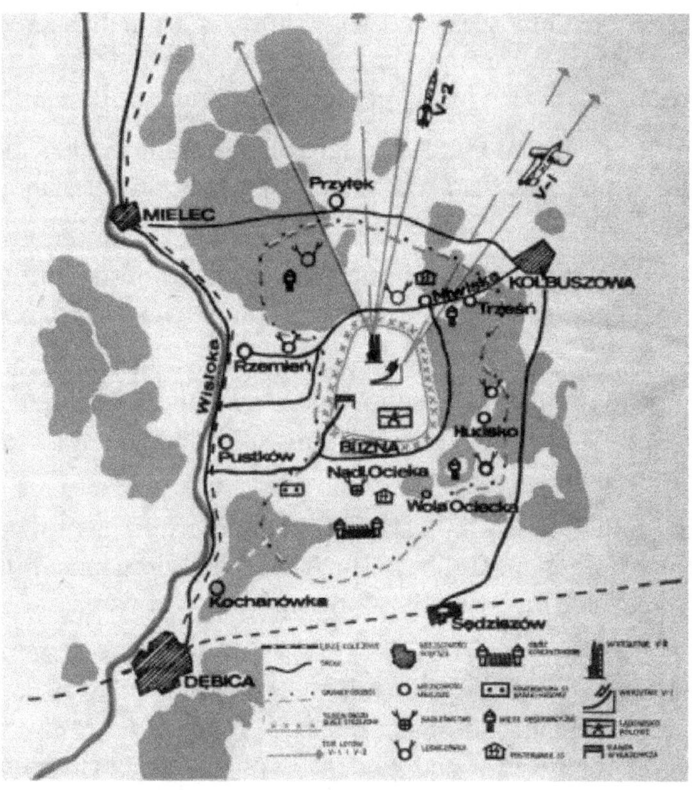

Map of Camp Heidelager and the launch paths of the missiles

Chapter Eleven

Meeting Alex

Colin provided a quick demonstration of how the cell phone worked. After asking questions of Colin, most of the men went back to their duties.

Jozef approached Colin with a man of about twenty with wild brown hair. He stretched out his hand. "Pleased to meet you, Lieutenant Colin. I'm Alex, one of your cousins. I'll show you around if you'd like."

Colin returned the handshake and followed Alex. "Colin, I'd like to ask you questions about what life is like in the future. I was a medical student at the University of Rzeszow when the war began, and of course, had to flee because of all the arrests."

"Arrests?" Colin asked.

"Right after the war, thousands and thousands of university professors, doctors, lawyers, and our top military officers from all over Poland were arrested and brought to a wilderness area similar to this one. And the Germans killed every one of them."

Colin suddenly felt like a rock was in his stomach. "But you escaped?"

Alex raised his shoulders and shrugged. "I was a nobody. Just a student, but the Germans closed all the universities and even the high schools. The Germans don't want their Polish subjects to be educated or influential because those people are the leaders of any country or uprising. The educated—not the working class or peasants—are feared because they would speak out and stand against those who attempt to take over a country."

Colin thought back to his favorite shirt that hung in his closet back home. Even Grandma, who was once a teacher, thought it was pretty funny. Now those words on the shirt's front, "School is Important, but Hockey is *Importanter*," did not seem so humorous anymore.

"My dad's a doctor. Poland will need doctors like him after the war, so you can always go back to school, Alex."

"I suppose anything's possible, but we'll still be fighting for our freedom if the Russians occupy this area. Nothing good ever comes when the Russians are in control." Alex pointed to a short path and signaled for Colin to follow. "Come down this way, and you can see our hideout."

They stopped in front of a pile of pine boughs on the ground, and Alex bent down to remove them. He then pulled back a tarp and a door that had been set on top. "Look, down there. This is where we hide at night or if it is raining hard. We even keep a little stove down there."

"Can I go down there?" Colin asked.

"Be my guest."

Colin sat on the tarp-lined floor and imagined what it must be like to sleep in this hole in the ground. He stretched out and determined that maybe only three or four men could fit. Even then, it would be a tight fit for sleeping.

"We stay in these dugouts during the winter. Sometimes we hide in friendly farmers' barns, but it's actually warmer in these holes."

"What do you eat? Do you hunt?" Colin asked.

"Sometimes we trap rabbits or other small animals, but shooting our guns might alert the Germans, so our food sources are limited. Many of the locals set out food on branches, bottles of milk, bread in sacks, things like that. They tie a white cloth on a tree near the barn if it is safe to approach their house, and they feed us what they can. Everyone has so little, but these villagers basically starve themselves so we can eat."

"Babcia says she and Maria are the eyes and ears of your army, and I guess they're your cooks too."

"Couldn't get along without people like them, Colin. You do know the Germans will shoot them if the locals are found to be helping the partisans or hiding Jews?" Alex raised his eyebrows and diverted his gaze. "Not only them but their entire family. It happens all the time, and the villagers are scared, but they still help us."

"Are there any Jews hiding around here?" Colin asked.

"Likely, but that information stays a closely guarded secret. Even neighbors don't know because there are a few who would turn the rescuers in for money. Besides, the Germans moved most of the Jews to ghettos and camps."

Colin hesitated, knowing his question might not provide the answer he wanted to hear. "Did you do anything to help the Jews?"

"You weren't here when it happened, so it's difficult to explain. Most of the Jews in this area don't speak Polish. They speak Yiddish. They dress differently and stay to themselves. Neither the Poles nor the Jews associated with each other except on business and lived in two different worlds. The Jews have been around here for hundreds of years, and it was always that way. Different places of worship, different schools, a whole different culture. But we got along most of the time—until the Germans showed up."

"So, you did nothing to help them?"

"Like I said, you had to be here to understand. The Germans took over our towns and villages, our government, our schools—almost immediately. Everything! Our soldiers fought back when Poland was first attacked, but the Germans had better tanks and airplanes that showered bombs all around here. Everyone was terrified after the Nazis killed hundreds of our people in the fighting."

"Uncle Jozef tried to tell us some of these things, but it's so hard to imagine," Colin said.

"After the Germans had complete control, our only hope was just to survive until the English and French rescued us, but that help never came. One man in our nearby town shot a German soldier on the street, and the Nazis pulled out the first ten Polish men who were standing nearby and shot them dead, right in front of everybody. Then, they took the names of ten others and put them on a placard, announcing that they would be shot if another German was killed. We knew the Germans were absolutely serious when we saw the bodies of innocent people on the street."

Colin glanced down at his AK pin. "Now I'm sort of embarrassed Captain Batory gave me this pin and the title of honorary lieutenant. After hearing these stories, I don't feel like I deserve this."

"I don't think you understand what you've given us. These new missiles are like nothing anyone has ever seen, and that includes the ones the English and Americans might have. It's a new weapon and has everyone baffled. All we find are blown-up fragments of the rockets here and there."

"So, what are you hoping to find that would solve the mystery of these missiles?" Colin asked.

"The best we could hope for is to find a fully intact, unexploded missile. I have no idea how we could ever get anything that huge out of here, but that's what the Home Army wants."

They turned in the direction of a distant whistling sound. "Looks like you and I need to get back to the others. Follow me through this shortcut, but watch out for the low branches. It's your turn to tell me about life in America."

Colin and Alex talked and trekked through the unbeaten path to the unit. "Colin, maybe you could return someday to see the fake village the Germans built. You might even get a distant view of one of the launch sites. It's about a mile walk in that direction. Are you up for that?"

Colin's face beamed with a wide smile. "I'll try to talk Uncle Jozef into letting me come. Thanks, Alex."

Chapter Twelve

Convincing Uncle Jozef

On his trek home with Uncle Jozef and Father Kurek, Colin bounced with excitement at the prospect of another great adventure.

"Colin, you can't come with me while I'm working as a forester for the Germans. I don't just sit in the forest waiting for things to happen. My job is hard work. If I lose this position, I'll be sent to Germany to work in one of their ammunition factories. Then who would take care of my family?"

Father Kurek detected the disappointed look on Colin's face. "Jozef, how about if Colin rides with me on my bike? I'm supposed to visit Debica tomorrow, and that road takes me close to that area. No one will see him on the back of my bicycle."

Colin sprinted up to hug Father Kurek, but in his excessive enthusiasm, accidentally knocked him to the ground. "Oh, man! I didn't mean to knock you down." Colin stretched out his hand to help the priest back up to his feet.

Father Kurek blew out a deep breath and dusted off his robes. "My, you're a powerful young man. Takes me back to the wrestling tournaments we had in high school!"

"I'm so sorry, Father. Colin will need to be more careful. He usually doesn't throw his full weight around at home, only with Adam when they get into their wrestling matches."

"Please, Uncle Jozef? Can I go? If I'm going to be of more help, I need to see these missiles with my own eyes." Colin smoothed his jacket and shorts to demonstrate he was worthy and held his breath in expectation.

Jozef put his hands in his jacket pocket and stared up into the heavens. "How can I say no to a first lieutenant?" He then broke out into a wide smile. "I know Father Kurek will take care of you. Just remember all the safeguards I've taught you."

The three walked up to the front of the house, and Noah started up with his usual guard dog barking.

"No, Noah. Stay back!" Colin yelled. "Don't worry. He doesn't jump on people, but our little one inside is crazy."

They entered the gate, and Colin ran ahead to hold onto Noah, but the dog nudged closer. "He wants you to pet him."

Father Kurek reached out his hand and stroked Noah's entire length. "My, this is a HUGE dog!" The priest smiled as Noah continued to press in on him for more attention. When Father Kurek leaned down, Noah licked his cheek and startled the poor priest.

"I've been christened by a dog!" Father Kurek laughed.

"This is the calm one, Father Kurek," Colin said. "Just wait until you meet Leia!"

"Noah and Leia? Do you name all of your animals after people in the Bible?" Father Kurek asked.

"When I was little, we had a bird named Boaz and our other dog that died was Goliath, but Leia is named after Princess Leia from *Star Wars*!"

"Star Wars?" Father Kurek grinned and shook his head. "Americans are interesting people."

Elise was near the entrance and holding Leia in her arms when she caught sight of Colin and Jozef. She jumped up and down and put Leia on the ground to run to her brother. "You're safe!"

"It was great, and I got to meet all the men in the unit. I'm part of the unit now. Look at this!" Colin pointed to the medal he wore on his soccer jersey and stretched the shirt out for her to get a better look.

"Is this the Elise I've heard so much about?" Father Kurek asked.

"Hello, Father Kurek!" Elise exclaimed.

"Let's pretend I'm one of the people who can't see you. May I touch the top of your head?" As he closed his eyes, Father Kurek put forth his hand and instantly found strands of wavy hair. "Now, tell me what you look like."

"I have lightish, brownish hair, and glasses. And that's about all."

The priest placed his hands on Elise's shoulders. "I can determine much more by just touching your shoulders. You are just a wisp of a young lady, but your muscles seem strong. Am I correct?"

"Watch this!" Elise proceeded to do a backbend, a perfect cartwheel, and a pirouette.

"Father, Elise is amazing. It's like having a circus performer from the fairs on market day. Elise is constantly moving and dancing. She's incredibly talented. Can you see why we love her so much?" Jozef said.

"So much is a mystery. How is it that people who are not their blood can neither see nor hear the dogs and Noah's loud barking?"

"They are so fortunate! Noah barks at every squirrel, horse, or car that goes by our house, and not one person or animal stops or pays any attention," Jadwiga said.

Maria leaned down to pet Noah. "But Mamma, he's a wonderful guard dog and so sweet and protective of us all. He loves us even if we don't always appreciate his sense of duty toward us."

"Noah and Leia are part of our family back at home. Maybe that explains it!" Colin said.

Everyone nodded in agreement.

Adam sat to rest with Noah and nuzzled him. "Too bad we can't hitch him to the cart. He could probably pull us all the way to town."

Jozef laughed. "Well, Noah, sorry you have to stay outside. Elise and Colin tell me you like to steal food from the table back at home. Naughty doggie!"

"What about this little one?" Father Kurek asked.

Maria picked up the chubby little Corgi. "Oh, she's a feisty one too, but she just melts into our arms when she sees we are upset or nervous. Such a sweetheart."

Jadwiga signaled for everyone to enter. "Dinner is ready. Father Kurek has to leave soon to return back to Kolbuszowa, so we can't wait much longer."

After dinner, the family all rose to receive Father Kurek's blessing before he departed.

On his way out the door, the priest whispered to Colin, "We need to talk about tomorrow morning."

Father Kurek put his arm around Colin's shoulder. "I'll be here early in the morning with my bike. It's getting pretty old and rusty, but you can ride on the back."

"So, we're going to that fake village tomorrow, Father Kurek?"

"You bet! I know exactly where it is!"

Chapter Thirteen

The Mystery Village

Stones and broken branches crackled under the tires as Father Kurek and Colin plodded along the narrow path leading to the fake village. The beginning of the journey wasn't as difficult because of the paved access road. Now, on the forest path, Colin could sense every bump and jostle and now marveled at how his father had once biked across the entire country during his college years.

Father Kurek leaned forward and put his hands on Colin's shoulders. "Are you getting tired yet? We can switch places."

"Not really, but we can stop for a drink of water." Colin sympathized with the priest's difficulty, holding on for dear life on the back of the bike.

Now off the bike, they both stretched and then arched their backs to help relieve the aches. Out of the corner of his eye, Colin saw what appeared to be a wild animal racing down the road toward them. Alarmed, they scurried into a clearing in a row of beech trees in hopes the beast wasn't pursuing them. Peering from behind the tree, Colin saw it wasn't a strange animal, but Noah galloping at breakneck speed.

"Oh, you stupid dog!" muttered Colin under his breath.

Noah put on his dog brakes and leaped to the grove of trees where Colin and the priest stood frozen. His tail wagging, he only wanted to be certain his favorite person was safe.

"Ugh, I must have left the gate open, and you were worried about me. You probably ran all that way." Colin knelt beside Noah and embraced him. "What do we do now, Father Kurek?"

It didn't take long before Noah snuffled up to Father Kurek. "Okay, okay, Noah." The priest looked up and down the deserted path. "We can walk the rest of the way for you to get a peek at the village. There's a short rope in my satchel for a leash. Can you hold onto Noah with it?"

The three trudged down just a short distance when Father Kurek detected a clearing in the woods. "Here it is, Colin. The Nazi's empty village."

They crouched down to view about seven shabby wooden houses. It all looked real enough, but no humans were in view. The white curtains flapped in the breeze through the open windows painted blue, and men's shirts and ladies' dresses hung on the clothesline behind each home. Standing next to each shed were what appeared to be the silent statues of cows, goats, and chickens. A cart loaded with hay seemed to be waiting for a horse and its owner to materialize.

"Why did the Germans build this phony village?" Colin asked. "It makes no sense."

"I agree… it does appear to be a big waste of time, but the Allies have been flying over these areas, probably to take photos from the air. It's all a Nazi trick. The Germans know the Allies won't drop bombs down on their missile facility and launch pads if people are living here. The Americans and English aren't barbarians like the Nazis. The German brutes showed no hesitation in sending bombs down on our houses at the beginning of the war."

"I still don't understand the difference between a Nazi and an SS guy and the Germans. They all seem the same."

"There is a difference, but to *us*, there's none. Almost all these men are Germans, but a Nazi is a member of the German socialist political party. This entire camp is swarming with Germans who are also the SS. The SS started out as Hitler's bodyguards but now oversee intelligence and policing and eliminating anyone they consider inferior or undesirable. That includes the Jews and us. The Jews were first, but the Polish people are next."

Colin looked perplexed. "You know a lot about the partisans. Why were you with them yesterday?"

"Didn't your Uncle Jozef tell you? I am not only a chaplain for the Home Army, but I'm also a partisan. The Germans think I'm just biking to see my parishioners who are scattered far and wide, but I'm also working to gather intelligence and missile fragments."

Colin's eyes lit up at the thought of a priest also being a soldier. Noah then laid down on Colin's side with his tongue hanging out as he took deep, agonizing breaths. "Noah is panting hard. He's really overheated. Is there some water nearby?"

"We all need some water. It's not far from here."

Father Kurek guided the bike in the direction of the pond, and Noah sped toward the water and greedily helped himself to a long drink. All at once, Colin and Father Kurek's attention shot up to the heavens where they detected a loud whistle that soon magnified into a roar. Before they could react, a falling missile sailed in their direction. The powerful blast propelled both Father Kurek and Colin into the nearby pond. Dazed, Colin sat up in the water and looked around. Right beside him, he saw the priest face down.

Noah paddled furiously to Father Kurek and pulled him from the pond onto the dry ground. The priest laid on his back for a few moments and opened his eyes to Noah, fervently licking him all over his face.

Colin plodded out of the water to assist Father Kurek, but Noah already had the rescue under control. The priest shielded his face from any more dog kisses and then affectionately pulled Noah onto his soaking wet clothing and hugged him.

Figure 1 V-2 Missile in Blizna during WWII

"Saved by dog kisses. What a great beast you are, Noah!" Father Kurek sat to survey the situation and was mystified by the heavy smell of alcohol all around. "Colin, do you smell that? That's the odor of the fuel from a V-2!" After adjusting his slightly bent glasses, the priest gazed in the direction of the crash.

Father Kurek's intuition as a partisan sprang into immediate action. "Colin, this is our chance to collect missile fragments." Colin rushed around the area and felt like a squirrel gathering nuts as he scurried about capturing a few of the valuable shiny missile fragments. A metal box in the crook of an oak tree caught his attention. He held up the unusual rectangular piece with dangling wires and then found another with switches on the nearby ground.

"These are just the kind of things I saw in my diagrams!"

The two hurried about, examining the parts when Colin reached into his pockets. His cell phone was gone!

"Father Kurek, we have to look for my cell phone. It might be in the water!"

"Let's first look around the ground. It might be impossible to find it in the water."

They frantically dashed from tree to tree to find the critical device. Tears began to flow from Colin's eyes, but he then noticed Noah sniffing a nearby bush. Colin sprinted to join his dog and noted the sun's light was reflecting off a shiny object. There, sitting beside a crumpled piece of shrapnel from the missile, was the cell phone.

"Another miracle!" Father Kurek shouted as he fell to his knees.

They stuffed their bags with the most intriguing missile fragments and sped home on the bicycle, which now had bent handlebars, while Noah kept pace at their side.

Chapter Fourteen

Adam's Burden

Colin unloaded the bulging bags onto the table inside the house. Jozef was mesmerized by the types of parts Colin and Father Kurek had retrieved.

Father Kurek looked very different in Jozef's tattered old clothing he had borrowed so his could dry. "Look here, Adam. Have you ever seen anything like these pieces Colin and I found? Look at this one with these small, twisted wires and this one with the smallest metal parts."

Adam shrugged and turned away as he walked out the back door. "I'm going outside to give the chickens some more water."

"What's up with Adam? He's even moodier than usual lately," Colin remarked.

"I know how he feels." Elise slouched back in the rocking chair. "All Adam and I do is stay around the house all day. It's hot and soooo boring! Colin gets to have all the fun."

"Getting blown into the water wasn't a bit of fun, Little Missy." Colin glared at Elise and pressed his lips together in a sarcastic manner. "Father Kurek almost drowned!"

Father Kurek sat next to Colin at the table. "I understand what your sister is talking about. You've become quite the celebrity and hero around here because you're the guy with the cell phone. Not that you're not important, but Elise and Adam's lives must seem pretty ordinary compared to yours."

Jadwiga stirred the potatoes and cabbage in the large metal pot and then brought it to the table. "You two may not understand how Adam suffers. His melancholy spirit is the same as many of the men in our family. I told you children that my husband took his life right after the Great War ended, but you may not know that Adam was just five-years-old when he found his Uncle Roman. Another suicide."

All the adults became silent and lowered their eyes.

Elise looked at their sad faces but couldn't contain herself. "Why? Why did they kill themselves?"

Father Kurek embraced Elise's hands. "Dear one, perhaps they lost their purpose in life and continuing on was too painful. I've listened to so many people confess the temptation to take their own life. It tears me up inside to hear the sorrow and see the tears of those so desperate with this deep feeling of hopelessness. Jadwiga's husband and son were surrounded by all this love, and God's love, yet they still took their own lives."

Jadwiga stood at the head of the table. "My husband, Jan, failed to see that the situation after the war might improve but didn't live to see that things did get better. Jan could never clearly see solutions to his problems, which were only temporary. Back then, he thought we lost our farm, but the new government eventually gave everyone's property back to them. My husband was dead when that happened."

Maria walked to the chest and removed the tattered album of photos and set it on the table. "This was Roman in his soldier's uniform. Look how handsome he was. That gorgeous black hair and his sparkling eyes. The girls, how they chased after him. They giggled and flirted when he walked by. All the young women wanted to be my best friend so they could be closer to Roman."

Jadwiga studied Roman's photos and passed them around the table. "But they didn't know how he struggled after the war. When he returned, Roman wasn't the same. He had these debilitating headaches. They were so bad that Roman couldn't think clearly and struggled to put his sentences together. He couldn't find joy anywhere, and loud noises, laughter, and music made his headaches worse. The same things that made everyone else happy drove Roman into taking his own life."

Jozef lamented. "Roman wanted to be free of his troubles, to escape from his misery and suffering. His death may be one reason why Adam, at times, suffers from feeling so depressed. Suicide might end the problems of the one who died, but Roman left us all with unbearable grief and overwhelming sadness."

Jozef knelt on the floor in front of Elise. "You and Colin are so different. So full of life, so much happiness, and kindness. It must be hard for you to understand how Adam feels."

Father Kurek sat pensively. "Sometimes we think everyone else's life is so much easier than our own. Men and women, boys, girls; we all struggle in different ways."

Chapter Fifteen

Elise's Plot

Cool breezes wafted through the back door of the old house that early summer morning. Colin, Elise, and Adam sat quietly around the table enjoying their morning soup. Breakfast was always the same, but Great-Grandpa Andrzej often managed to find extra food to add to their morning soup.

"Grandpa Andrzej sure knows how to outsmart the Germans, doesn't he? I wonder how he managed to find these eggs?" Elise asked.

Colin added a few more chunks of bread to his broth. "That's crazy how the Germans expect his hens to lay a certain amount of eggs, and Grandpa Andrzej has to buy some on the black market if his hens don't produce enough."

"Your grandpa has to give an accounting of how many eggs his chickens laid when he brings them to the produce and egg collection center, but he hides some for us. He tells the Germans his chickens are old and that they're not laying very many anymore," Adam said.

"Those chickens with black pom-poms on their heads are the strangest ones I've ever seen. It must be hard for them to walk without running into each other." Elise jumped up and pretended to be one of the hens bumping into chairs.

Adam smirked at his cousin's silliness, and Elise smiled back. Now that she understood him better, Elise desperately wanted to make Adam happy.

"Where's this food collection center, Adam?" Colin inquired.

"It's right next to the grain mill near the manor house. Most of the food comes from the farms all around here that are run by the Germans. They send a lot of it back to Germany. Poland's now what they call 'Germany's breadbasket.' They make tanks and guns in Germany; we grow their food. That's Hitler's master plan."

Elise crouched over her bowl and then tilted her head. "Are there lots of soldiers there to guard the food?"

"Not really, Babcia and my mother go in there a few times every day to get food to cook for the officers' meals. Anyway, no one would dare to steal. There are so few of us villagers around anymore. I guess the Germans don't worry about theft." Adam stood and placed his bowl on the cupboard. "I'll go pump some water to wash the bowls."

Elise walked over to the place on the floor where Maria kept the wash pan and set it on one end of the table. She then retrieved an apron from the hook and slid it over her head. The apron reminded her of the times she spent with her own grandmother baking cookies or a pie.

"Colin, would you bring over the kneading board and the crock with the dough?" Elise watched as her strong brother lifted both onto the table. "The dough is probably ready for its second round of kneading."

"I can help you with the kneading when your arms get tired," Colin offered.

Adam staggered in with two pails of water and set them on the floor near the basin.

Elise stood on the stool to reach the tin box filled with flour.

Adam ran up to retrieve the tin. "Here, let me get that for you. I'm taller."

"Thanks, Adam. Hey, stay here for a minute to help me figure out that food area near the mill." Elise opened the lid and scooped out a handful of flour and spread it on the board. "Use your finger on the flour to draw a map of that mill, sort of like if a bird was looking down at it."

Adam smirked, "Okay, but you must be really bored." He drew a rectangle and began to add details. "This is the granary, and here are the doors. This is where they keep the bags of flour, to the left is where fruits are kept, and in the corner is where they store vegetables and eggs. To the right of the granary is a shed where they smoke the meats. They have hundreds hanging in the smokehouse. Best smell in the world."

"Where are the kitchens where Babcia and Maria work?" Colin asked.

Adam drew an arrow to show the path to the kitchens. "They're over here. They do some work inside the big house, but the hot cooking during the summer is done over here, next to the smokehouse."

"It wouldn't be that hard to sneak in and steal a little food, would it?" Elise asked.

"Are you kidding? Impossible!" exclaimed Adam. "First, the Germans would see the food you're bringing out."

"How about if I just put some inside my pockets?" Colin asked.

Elise clapped her hands. "The rucksacks are invisible on me, remember?"

"Even if that did work, there are the dogs. Not nice ones like Noah and Leia but killer dogs the Germans use in their patrols."

Elise put her hands on her hips. "I would make them behave. I trained Noah and Leia to sit and stay."

"That's not the same. These are German Shepherd dogs. They could rip you to shreds."

"Maybe those dogs can't see me either." Elise flipped her hair out of her eyes. "It was just a thought."

🌲🌲🌲

Elise couldn't let go of her idea of being more useful to the family. Each night, they complimented her bread, even though it was never as high or light as Maria's. Jozef always said Elise's loaves were what bread must taste like in heaven, but Elise was certain he would have said that even if her bread fell totally flat.

That night at the evening meal, Elise listened to the adult conversation, waiting for the right time to bring up the subject.

Jozef reached over for another slice of Elise's bread. "We have another unit moving into the area next week from Warsaw. They're hoping and just waiting for one of those V-2 missiles to not blow up into hundreds of pieces." He tore the bread up and dipped it into the rabbit stew. "Forty more men to feed."

The adults all shook their heads as they considered the impossibility of the task. Jadwiga exclaimed, "Lately, the Germans seem to be so skittish with the Russians pushing in from the east."

"Why are the Germans nervous?" Colin asked.

Joseph replied, "They must be getting the same news as we are about the Americans. Slowly, the American forces are working their way through France since they landed over a year ago, but, at this point in the war, nothing is certain. Germany could still win."

Elise looked up from her bowl of stew. "I have an idea. I can sneak into the granary and steal food for the partisans."

Jozef leaned forward and scowled. "No, that is impossible! Too dangerous! Where did you get such an idea?"

Elise cringed, as she had never seen Jozef angry and never at *her*, but she was resolute. "Father Kurek thinks Colin and I have been sent here on a mission. I would have never been sent if I wasn't meant to do more dangerous things. I'm not here to just cook and clean."

"I can't bear the thought of anything happening to you, Elise." Jozef was near tears. "The answer is no."

Colin bit his lip and muttered a few sounds before he exploded. "No one, especially me, wants to see anything bad happen to Elise, but I think her plan is a good one! We've seen lots of movies where the good guys do all sorts of spying and stealing to foil the enemy."

"That's all made up for a movie, Colin," Maria commented.

"I know, but if you watch these movies and read books about spies, you know that good will conquer evil…" Colin's voice trailed off. "And besides, you've let me do some pretty dangerous stuff, Uncle Jozef. Do you care more about Elise than me?"

Jozef's eyes lowered, and he blew out a deep breath. "No, of course not. I love you both in very different ways, but equally. It's just that Elise is a girl, and girls don't do those dangerous things like men do. I'm treating you like a man, Colin."

Adam couldn't contain himself. "What about our cousin Anna who was a Girl Guide? She learned to use a gun when she was Elise's age and now works in the Home Army as a courier. That job is as dangerous as yours, isn't it, Uncle Jozef? The Germans would kill her just like they would any man who they discovered."

"What's a Girl Guide, Aunt Maria?" asked Elise. "I used to be in Indian Guides with my dad, and I learned all sorts of neat things."

Maria grinned in amazement. "Maybe it's the same thing. Before the war, the Girl Guides would learn all sorts of useful things like first aid and survival skills, but things changed when the war started. Now they decipher and deliver messages to the underground and report German troop movement. The older ones in their twenties, like Anna, often fight alongside the men, blow up bridges, and run orphanages that hide and care for Jewish children."

"Wow! I want to be a Girl Guide. Just think of how helpful my being invisible would be for the Girl Guides!"

Jozef sat with his hands over his entire face and then rested his chin on his fists. "I'll talk to Anna first. Maybe we can invite her over to meet Elise." He kept shaking his head in disbelief, but then began to smile. "You, Miss Elise, are as remarkable as your brother. Who am I to stop the hand of God?"

Chapter Sixteen

Anna's Visit

"Anna's here! She's coming down the road," yelled Adam. "She's with Uncle Jozef!"

The three children ran to the door, their faces beaming with excitement. Elise's smile couldn't have been wider.

"Quit that bouncing, Elise. You want Anna to think you're grown up, don't you?" Colin yelled.

Anna waved her hands as she approached the house and then broke into a sprint. "I can see you! We are blood cousins for sure!" Noah bounded toward her, and she affectionately gave him a few seconds of love before she went into the house. She hugged all three children and then looked around. "Maria told me Elise keeps a very tidy house, and she's absolutely correct!"

Elise studied Anna from head to toe. She seemed so perfect with her dark black hair styled more fashionably than Maria's, and her polka-dotted dress was more modern. Maria and Jadwiga almost always wore headscarves that tied in the back. Elise concluded maybe the scarves were only for cooks in the kitchens.

"I have so many questions for you, Elise, but Father Kurek has already told me so much about you. You being visible to me will make it so much easier when we're working together. I haven't stopped thinking of the possibilities and how useful you might be."

"One thing we need to make certain, Elise. Are you sure you want to put yourself at risk like this?" asked Jozef.

"Oh, yes! Anna can teach me about how to be safe and all the details of her work. I can do it. I'll prove it to you!"

Anna embraced Elise's hands. "We are sisters now, not just cousins. The male partisans say they are brothers, and the women say 'sisters.' You, Elise, will make a very courageous and brave partisan!"

Elise couldn't resist bouncing on her heels. "When do I start?"

Everyone chuckled at Elise's exuberance.

Anna took Elise's hand and strolled to the table. "Let's sit down with Maria and Jadwiga and think this through first. Would this evening be too soon for your first mission?"

"How about right now?" Elise exclaimed.

The summer solstice sky was coaxing the sun to end the day when Maria and Elise arrived at the edge of the trees near the manor house. "Boy, that was a bumpy ride on the back of your bike. Good thing it didn't take *too* long."

"Is Jozef's rucksack too heavy for you?"

"No way! I plan on wearing that other one on my chest. That will mean twice as much food."

"Good girl! Let's go over this once more. I must stay in the woods with the bike, but you are to run to the granary as soon as you see Maria coming from the big house. She'll select the most important food for you to put in the sack and then you run back to me as quickly as possible. Remember—I'm standing near the tree with the big stork's nest. Got it?"

"Got it!" exclaimed Elise. "But, why is there only one soldier at the granary? He looks like he's resting. Not a very good guard, it seems to me."

"This is Sunday, and most everyone's at the villas in Pustkow. Many of the regular soldiers have visitors on Sunday, and they even have a movie theatre there. Most Sundays are pretty quiet. That's why we chose Sunday for your first mission."

After about twenty minutes, just as she promised, Maria strolled down the path, swinging two straw baskets. Trying not to look suspicious, she swayed her head rhythmically to the right and the left hoping to see if Elise was in place.

"Go!" Anna whispered. "God be with you."

Elise sauntered through the meadow, keeping the same pace as Maria to arrive at the same time. Once inside the granary building, she opened her sacks for Maria to place eggs, sausage, and cheese. The strong smell of garlic made her want to sneeze, but Elise managed to swallow each sneeze silently. Everything was going as planned. Maria tapped her on the head to signal she had finished, and Elise broke into a sprint to return to Anna.

Without warning, the sound of ferocious barking broke through the still summer air. Elise turned around and saw a huge black and brown German Shepherd darting in her direction, and a man was shouting. Elise thought *Everyone had been wrong! Dogs weren't like people, and this one can obviously see me!*

Elise's heart raced, and she continued to keep her eyes in Anna's direction as she ran. She couldn't waste one second to turn back to see the dog or the German soldier. Elise visualized the possibility of his razor-sharp teeth and massive jaw grabbing at her leg.

Then, the dog's barking became fainter and farther away, and Elise turned her head in the direction of that sound. At a distance, she saw the Shepherd pursuing a deer into the woods far away. As he reached the tree line, the dog halted and paced for a few seconds and then sauntered back to the granary where the angry soldier waited.

Elise ran into Anna's arms and sobbed, but then grabbed Anna's hand to lead her to the bike. "I'm okay, I'm okay," she panted. "We need to get out of here!"

Anna pedaled furiously and didn't stop until they arrived back home. After walking the bike through the gate, both she and Elise fell onto the small patch of dried grass in front of the house. Elise removed the rucksacks and laid on her back, exhausted but elated.

Anna stretched out next to Elise. "On one hand, that's the most dangerous mission I've ever been on, but as it turns out, we were pretty safe all along. It went like clockwork, didn't it, Elise?"

"Except for that dog. Are you sure it didn't see me?"

"I doubt it since I saw the whole thing. That dog was chasing after that deer from the start, and the soldier was probably angry the animal had broken his chain."

The boys ran out, and Colin rushed to Elise's side. "Are you okay? Your face is as red as a beet!"

Elise and Anna sat up and slowly got to their feet and walked with the boys. "Your sister was a real hero!" said Anna. "Wait until she tells you the frightening thing that happened!"

As they walked to the front door, Elise exuberantly relayed the story of the vicious dog to Adam and Colin. Both boys hugged and congratulated Elise for a job well done.

"Now I want to see what foods you managed to get." Anna lifted the sack onto the table. "You ran so fast with this heavy load? Remarkable!"

Elise pulled her shoulders back and grinned. "All the kneading and kitchen work has prepared me for this, I guess. Sort of like when the army guys have to do push-ups and pull-ups."

Anna's mouth dropped as she removed the foods from the sacks. "Cheese, smoked sausages—and lots of them—a few peaches, lard, even a few tins of fish. Remarkable!"

"Remarkable seems to be everybody's favorite word around here lately!" Colin said.

"These foods truly *are* remarkable and will be so helpful to our hungry soldiers. Those men often have to eat what they find in the forests." Anna began to sob, but her words choked through her tears. "These may even save someone from starvation. You may not know this, Elise and Colin, but everyone in this village has experienced near-starvation and severe hunger. There were many times all I thought of was food. I was always so hungry."

Elise rose to stand next to Anna and embraced her. "Elise, these two sacks are worth ten lives. You likely saved ten lives today by what only *you* could do. Remarkable!"

Figures 2 Hupka Manor House and old Granary in Niwiska

Chapter Seventeen

Noah's First Adventure

"You'll be okay, Noah. You're just as brave and tough as Elise and Colin." Adam sat next to Noah on the worn porch step. "You'll be home in less than an hour, and Babcia said she'd even give you a big chunk of that sausage if you bring enough back home."

Adam observed Anna's bicycle rounding the corner, and scurried into the house to announce her arrival. Elise was already equipped with her rucksacks and fastened her hair into a ponytail with a red ribbon.

"Children, do you think Noah is ready for his first Home Army adventure?" Anna asked as she entered. "Let me see that sack for Noah your Babcia made from your blanket, Elise."

Colin pulled Anna by the hand to bring her out back to where Noah was laying. "Look at the straps and snaps to tie the bag to his back and around his legs and his collar. It fits perfectly, and these sides are like saddlebags."

"I was going to say 'remarkable,' but I'll use another word. How about 'ingenious'? This blanket saddlebag is an *ingenious* invention!" Anna exclaimed. "One more thing before we go, Colin. You and Elise are both young partisans in the Home Army, and so you'll each need a codename."

"A codename?"

"Yes, all partisans have one, and officers like Captain Batory often have five or ten. We must change them if anyone we deem suspicious finds out."

"Do you have one?" Colin asked.

"Yes, but only those in our unit are to know. I am 'Teacher.' Does that fit me?"

"I thought you told me you were forced by the Germans to be a cook at the villas for the officers in Pustkow," Elise said.

"Before the German occupation, I was studying to be a teacher, to teach children your age, but that all ended." Anna's eyes saddened. "Alex, my fiancé, was studying to be a doctor. His studies also ended when the war started."

"Alex! I met a guy named Alex. He's in my unit!" Colin exclaimed.

"Yes, that's him. We hope to be married when the war ends."

Elise looked at Anna quizzically. "So, are you still going to be a teacher someday?"

"Alex and I plan to attend school together when we are married. For now, we only live for the war to end." Anna folded her arms. "Let's get back to deciding your codenames. How would you like to be known by your unit?" Anna asked.

"I know! I want to be 'Firecracker'!" Elise exclaimed.

Anna broke into a hearty laugh. "Firecracker sounds like a scary enough name. How about you, Colin?"

Colin lowered his eyes and kicked at some of the dry dirt. "How about 'Goon'? I liked being the goon in hockey."

"I have no idea what a goon is, but sure," said Anna. "Those are perfect! Everyone will know who Goon and Firecracker are!" Anna declared. "Just perfect!"

"What about Noah? Shouldn't he have a name?" Elise asked.

"Let me suggest a few names." Anna tapped her fingers against her chin and stared intently at Noah. How about 'The Giant' or maybe 'Protector'?"

"Protector's a perfect name!" Elise yelled. Colin snickered and just bobbed his head for approval. "What about Leia? Shouldn't she also have a name?"

Colin snickered. "How about 'Pampered Pup' for a codename?

"Colin, Leia's brave in her own way!" Elise protested.

"One more thing—Captain Batory gave me something to give to you, Elise." Anna knelt in front of her and pinned a medal to Elise's shirt. "You are now an honorary second lieutenant in the Home Army. Captain Batory said you deserve to be a first lieutenant, but he must request that pin from his superiors. This one will have to suffice until then."

Elise caressed her pin and did a celebratory cartwheel.

Anna reached into her other pocket. "There's more! A Girl Guide badge for bravery. You are now an official Girl Guide, Elise! Girls like you and from all over Europe are serving their countries during the war because of the invaluable skills they learned as Girl Guides!"

Noah nuzzled Anna's skirt. "No badges for you, Noah, but maybe I could look around for something very special. Off we go, Firecracker and Protector!"

Elise climbed on the back of Anna's rickety bike, and the two pedaled off with Noah keeping pace, like a well-trained military dog. Just a month ago, Noah was a minimally disciplined dog whose stomach was his biggest downfall. He knew how to sit and lay down on command, but the seriousness of the present situation had transformed him. Now, Noah was constantly at attention for real danger and never let mere squirrels, horses, or the roar of trucks and cars affect him. It was like he had been listening to everyone's conversation and could discern between good and evil. He truly was the protector of his adopted family.

The bike's front tire coasted to the right and kept biting at the soft mud resulting from last night's downpour. None of this bothered Noah who effortlessly galloped along, his patchy tongue dangling from the side of his mouth. He was born to run. Noah didn't seem to mind that every part of his white fur was now brown.

Anna slowed her pace and signaled to Elise that it was time for them to dismount. She guided the bike to a grove of trees that were out of view from the granary. Elise fastened the blue saddlebag onto Noah and secured the snaps.

"Ready?" Anna whispered.

Elise knelt on the wet leaves beside Noah and embraced him. "It'll be okay, Noah. You just stay with me."

Just like the week before, Elise's timing was perfection. She guided Noah with a shortened rope to the granary when she saw Maria, and Elise and the dog stood next to her as they proceeded with their routine. Another expertly executed operation! Noah's bag carried the cheeses, real coffee, and the first pears and apricots of the season. Maria placed two packages of freshly cut up chicken and about eight rings of sausage in Elise's pack. All the foods were safely tucked inside.

Elise tugged on Noah's rope, and he began to trot back to the tree line to meet Anna. Abruptly, he paused, sniffed the air, and then dashed back to the smokehouse where hundreds of smoked bratwurst sausage links sat in the tub near the doors. Noah snatched a hefty link and galloped back to meet up with Elise.

The guard stared and then leaped to his feet and began to yell at the peculiar sight: a twelve-inch-long sausage flying in the air, hovering over the ground! He bolted into the meadow but came to a crashing halt as the image of the sausage faded into the woods. With his feet apart and hands on his head in amazement, the soldier just gazed into the woods.

On her way back to the house carrying a basket filled with foods for the evening meal, Maria spotted the soldier attempting to pursue the flying sausage. The soldier ran toward her and screamed, "Did you see that sausage dangling above the ground? It was traveling in the direction of the forest!"

Maria took a calming breath and shook her head. "No, I saw nothing. Point to where you saw it go. Which direction?"

"Ah! It's gone into the woods!" the soldier screamed as he pointed to the tree line.

"A sausage has gone into the woods?" Maria asked in a playful tone.

"I saw it with my own eyes! I'm sure of it!" The soldier started to tremble and held his hands to his cheeks, his voice beginning to crack. "I mean, I *think* I saw a sausage…"

"Sir, I saw nothing, but there are tales of strange beasts who roam the wilderness. The old folks say that some can change their form.

That sort of story has been reported in old tales since I was a little girl."

"I suppose beasts in the forests can play tricks," the baffled soldier agreed.

"Come to the kitchen. Jadwiga has prepared a wonderful plum kuchen. Maybe you just need to cool off for a while." Anna showed the soldier some of the foods in her baskets to distract him while they ambled down the path to the manor house.

That evening, Elise wasn't sure if she wanted to laugh at Noah or be angry with him, as his hungry impulses sometimes still ruled over him. All she knew was that his usual bowl of zurek now included chunks of tasty sausage.

Chapter Eighteen

The Spy

"I'm trying. I really am trying, but I haven't found any schedule the Germans left behind in the records." Colin powered down his cell phone. "Researching on the internet sucks the battery dry."

Jozef paced the floor as two other partisan foresters sat at the table and studied Colin's notes. "Maybe the Germans destroyed their records after they left, and there isn't anything for us to see. That's what a smart military operation does. They don't leave information behind."

"If we only knew when the Germans plan to launch the next V-2 in the next few weeks. Because of Colin's research, we know how to manipulate the radio and guidance system controls. Our men in the field surely will be able to retrieve the missile before the Germans," Alex said.

"If we only knew their schedule!" Colin said.

Elise, who had been sitting quietly on the bed, timidly approached the table. "Aunt Maria says the officers meet in Colonel Heiss' office every morning. Maybe I could be like a mouse in the corner and listen in."

All the men shook their heads and guffawed at her suggestions.

"I might overhear something useful. Don't you think it's at least worth a try?" Elise begged.

"How would you get into a closed-door meeting, Elise?" Alex asked.

Colin threw up his hands and raised his voice. "Alex, remember—Elise is invisible! She could just slip into the room when the door is open, maybe after Maria serves the officers lunch. Something like that."

Jozef kept shaking his head in disagreement. "I can't let Elise near those monsters. No, I won't allow it!"

Adam, who had been sitting away from the group, walked toward his uncle and put his hand on his shoulder. "Uncle Jozef, we've already tested what happens when Colin is near people who can't see him. There's nobody they can grab onto. They can't hurt Elise."

Jozef placed his hands over his mouth while he studied Elise's eager face. "Alright, if Elise is willing, she can go with Maria and my mother tomorrow."

Elise bounced up and down with excitement and then bounded over to hug Jozef. "I promise to be extra careful. Remember, I'm the one who's been close to the Germans while I was getting all that food for the soldiers… and Noah, too!"

Colin put his arm around his sister. "You don't have to be a man, or older, or a trained spy to make a difference, Elise. You only have to care enough about what's right and then be there. I'm proud of you!"

Jozef held Elise in front of him in amazement. "My darling Elise. You *are* my brave girl. Colin's right. We should never be afraid about these missions when it is the right thing to do."

Elise sat near the flower arrangement on the dining room table in the manor house that next morning. She occasionally laid back in weariness, wondering when the officers would arrive.

Maria shuttled cups and saucers back and forth between Colonel Heiss' office and the kitchen. She shot Elise the slightest smile every time she passed but never said a word. At any moment, a German or servant could have entered the area, so Maria needed to pretend Elise was non-existent. So far, the plan was working like a charm.

"Maria!" a voice bellowed from the second floor. Colonel Heiss' boots clicked as he walked across the black and white marble floor in the dining room. "There you are. Maria, some other officers from

Pustkow will be here promptly at ten o'clock. Instruct Thaddeus to wait at the door to escort them into my office."

"Yes, Colonel Heiss. I'll inform him right now." Maria walked into the kitchen to find the colonel's butler.

Elise jumped off the table and walked into Colonel Heiss' office after he entered. The German officer was mumbling to himself as he sat behind his massive mahogany desk. The room was large enough to also accommodate an enormous table with twelve chairs and a few upholstered sofas with coffee tables.

A lovely blonde woman with a neatly fitted navy blue suit arrived and approached the desk. "Colonel, I have a copy of the inventory of what the soldiers should start to crate up for our departure. Has a date been set?"

"I'll have a better idea when the officers from Warsaw arrive. Set the folder on my desk."

Elise took note of where the woman placed the folder and then heard the loud clumping of heels coming from the front entrance.

"Heil Hitler!" the officers barked while raising one arm to Heiss with the Nazi salute as they entered his office. Uncle Jozef hated that greeting and mockingly called it "howling with the wolves." Elise thought back to her school, where some silly boys would give each other the Nazi salute. She shook her head in disgust; those foolish kids didn't understand they were giving tribute to pure evil!

The SS officers gathered around the table, and Heiss sat at the head with his secretary at his side with her notepad. "Let's start with reports from the latest communications…"

Elise tried to make sense of the names of cities, people, and an endless litany of military jargon like "velocity, operational firings, and guidance systems." Their words were all coming to her in English, but they might as well have been in German considering she couldn't understand what they were talking about.

An officer with a bulldog-like face was the one who did the most talking from the papers sitting before him on the table. "Lately, the V-2 has been nothing but a failure with the site of the missile's impact falling far from its planned target. On the 28th of this month—an airburst, the 30th—a burn out, and then another guidance failure on the first of this month."

"So, Albrecht," Heiss said. "Reports are that Hitler rages into a near tantrum when he hears that his pet missile program is riddled with problems. The missiles might terrorize the people in London and Antwerp, but they haven't caused the damage that von Braun promised."

Elise now knew the man with the horrible face was named Albrecht. She couldn't stand to look at him as he continued. "Von Braun has sent word that all our records on the V-2 should be hidden far away from Blizna. Some of his men should arrive any day to gather them."

"When are the next launches scheduled?" Heiss asked.

Elise's ears perked up, and she raced to stand next to the man at whom the question was directed.

"I have one launch scheduled tomorrow in the direction of Sarnacki by the Bug River. For the next three days, we will launch a few hours after dawn. We have learned early morning is the most advantageous time, so our men have plenty of time to retrieve the fragments if there's a crash."

"I have no idea how the Poles manage to routinely beat us to the sites. The Home Army is swarming in the forests ready to pounce on the crash sites," Albrecht said.

Colonel Heiss scowled. "Men, we all know it is a matter of weeks, and then this program in Blizna will end. As soon as we get word of the Russians moving in, we'll begin our plans to blow up the remaining missiles and move anything of value to Germany."

"Colonel Heiss, we'll have no further need for those foresters, who I'm certain are working with the Polish partisans. Keep an eye out for their leaders, and we'll arrest them...*and* their families, right before we move out of Blizna," Albrecht asserted.

Heiss stood to end the meeting. "That will send a message to all the villagers who have been emboldened by their acts of sabotage.

These next three launches may be our last, and we want to frighten them—not cause a last effort revolt. Don't give them any hint that we are likely closing down the Blizna launch facility."

Chapter Nineteen

Espionage

As she ran home down the road from the manor house, Elise chanted "The next three days after dawn. The next three days after dawn." Heiss even confirmed the dates, so she knew this sentence was all she needed to report... *and* the other details about the foresters being in danger.

Colin and Adam sat on the front steps waiting for Elise's return. "Look! Colin, I think that might be Elise!" Her faraway colorful image came into view, and they soon heard the pounding of her shoes. Both dashed to meet up with her.

"Tomorrow. The officers said the next three days right after dawn."

"Climb up on my shoulders, and I'll give you a piggy-back ride home!" Colin stooped down for Elise to grab onto her brother's shoulders, and she wrapped her legs around his waist.

Elise yawned in exhaustion. "Hurry! I need water!"

"Tomorrow! We can't wait for Uncle Jozef to come back home. Colin, we have to take Elise to the unit right now so she can report what she heard!" Adam filled up their canteens with water and put his knife and a loaf of bread in his knapsack.

"Adam, are you going with us?" Colin asked.

"I'll come with you part of the way, but Uncle Jozef might be angry if I turn up at their hideout." Adam stood in front of Elise. "I'll help Elise watch the forest floor and fight off any wild animals with my knife."

Elise smiled at Adam, but Colin didn't seem to understand Adam's strong desire to be part of their adventures. "Colin, Adam wants to make this sacrifice. He's had to sit home while you and I go out on these missions."

"But Adam, *you're* the one in danger, not us." Colin shrugged. "It's all up to you."

"Let me leave a note for Maria. I'll tell her not to worry." Colin scribbled his message on a piece of paper and placed it inside the broom handle where the secret messages were kept.

"Do you need to rest some more, Elise? We can wait a little while longer if you need to," Adam inquired.

"No, I'm good. Let's get moving!"

The three collected a few eggs for the soldiers from the chicken coop and then scuttled off into the woods, always checking to see if any Germans or partisans were nearby.

The hidden path was tucked away in the depths of Blizna's forest, and it swerved back and forth in an unpredictable manner. Adam placed Elise between him and Colin. "Elise, you follow your brother, but watch your step with these gnarly tree roots and stones."

Elise's mind was filled with colorful imagery of what she thought the inside of the partisan's forest would look like: exploding grenades, machine gun bursts with bullets flying, and soldiers standing with their rifles aimed in all directions. So far, the wilderness seemed ordinary, like one of the national parks back in America.

"Adam, you probably need to go back now." Colin gave his cousin a quick hug. "I sure wish you could come all the way with us, but even if Uncle Jozef weren't upset, the other partisans would be angry if an outsider knew their location."

"Yeah, I get it." Adam's voice dropped off, and he lowered his head. "Sure wish we could change places. You two are so lucky."

Adam retraced his footsteps as he meandered on the path back to his home.

Elise followed closely behind Colin as they continued on. "I don't hear any noises yet."

"They don't make much noise, Elise. They're probably sitting around or are on sentry duty or going through drills to stay in good fighting form."

"I thought the hideout would be more exciting than that."

"It's NOT like those movies you see on TV!"

Farther down, Colin spotted a tree trunk laying over their path. "That's probably their sign." He ran up to it and rolled it over to find the white painted cross on the bottom. "We turn right and go through these trees. It's just a mile away."

Colin pointed to a grove of beech trees. "As we get closer, we have to move slowly until we're certain it's safe." He detected movement ahead and began to croak like a frog. Then, he picked up a stick and began to hit the tree trunks between his croaks. Deciding it was safe to approach, Colin called out, "It's the Goon!"

Jozef shot up to his feet and looked in their direction and waved. Elise ran into his arms. "Uncle Jozef! I did it. I found out a whole bunch of stuff for your unit!"

"Brothers, for those of you who are her kin and can see her, this is Miss Elise, my precious girl." Jozef signaled for the children to rest on the log. "Tell us what you've discovered."

"I was right there in Colonel Heiss' office. They didn't see a thing!"

"Good to know you're not related to any Nazis!" Alex declared.

"A man with a face like a mean bulldog said there'd be launches for the next three days in a row."

"Elise must have seen Albrecht! That man walks like he's sitting on a bulldog, too!"

"He said the launches would be right after dawn, and they would be aiming them near a town near a bug river. I wrote the name of the area on my arm with Heiss' big messy ink pen. Look here."

Elise held out her arm to show the men the word "Sarnacki" written over her entire forearm.

"Sarnacki, near the Bug River! Elise, you're a genius!"

"Was there anything else?" Jozef asked.

"They were upset that you guys always seemed to get to the crash sites before they did. One more scary thing: they're getting ready to move out of Camp Heidelager and said they don't have any use for the foresters anymore and will arrest the leaders soon. Their families too."

"We need to get word to the remaining villagers. They'll need to go into hiding soon."

Colin nudged his sister. "Elise heard about some guy with the last name of some color who wants all the records of the V-2 taken from Camp Heidelager and hidden somewhere else."

"Von Braun! He's one of Hitler's top scientists who first created the ideas for these missiles," Jozef said.

After Elise reported the most important details, she went back into her mind to recall the meeting step by step.

"Let me get this information to Captain Batory so he can assign men to the Sarnacki region." Jozef put his supplies in his rucksack and signaled Colin and Elise to come with him. "Can you two get back to the house on your own? I need to bike to headquarters."

Colin and Elise grinned, unbothered by the dangers that plagued everyone else. "Uncle Jozef, no problem! We found our way here, AND we're invisible!"

Captain Albrecht inspecting the training ground of
Camp Heidelager.

Chapter Twenty

Codename Motyl: The Next Mission

The mid-July rains had no pity, and Jozef's usually dry path now resembled a shallow river. Each step required greater effort as he trudged down the grassy edges of the road leading to the forester station.

The sudden rustle of leaves then alerted him. "Jozef! It's me, Marek," was all he heard. Marek's nest-like hair camouflaged his presence in the grove of trees.

Jozef glanced up and down the road and was confident there were no signs of Germans, so he slipped into the woods to join his fellow partisan. "I was hoping to find you." Jozef reached into his pouch and handed his friend some cheese and two loaves of bread. "Here, one loaf for you, and one for the others."

"Your family lives closer to the gates of heaven than any other I know." Marek ripped off a chunk, savoring the scent of homemade bread, and then bit into it. "I've some important news for you. Partisans found an unexploded missile near the Bug River. Headquarters wants you and Colin to come with us to hand it off to the English, but we have to wait until the skies have stopped with all this cursed rain."

"I can't leave my position at the forestry station for any overnight missions. You know that!"

"All I know is Batory asked for Colin to be there with his phone and of course, that would include you also coming."

Jozef tipped his head back and briefly closed his eyes. "I can't just leave my mother and sister all alone. The Nazis would be swarming my house if I didn't show up for work."

"I could always accompany Colin without you, but this operation promises to be big and may be your only chance to see the kind of action we all dream about."

"That's a long ride for Colin on the back of a bike. I don't know…" Jozef's voice trailed off, and he looked to the ground.

"When all this rain stops, most of us will bike to a beet field, but you two will ride with old Andrzej on a potato cart. That field is where we'll hand over the missile parts to the Allies."

Jozef's heart pounded. "How in the world will the English get the missile parts from a beet field?"

"By plane, but I'll explain the details later. The Russians will be pushing into this area within weeks, and we can't let them get their hands on these missiles. Are you in?"

"I gave my word to fight for Poland's freedom, didn't I?"

"One more thing, Batory wants the dog to come too. He'll ride on top of the potatoes."

Jozef rubbed the back of his neck and chuckled. "This is either going to be the most exciting military operation in history, or we're all going to die."

Marek patted his friend on the back. "We'll station some men around your house and get your family to safety if there are problems. We'll leave around July 20th. For now, all you need to know is 'Motyl,'—the codename for our mission."

Chapter Twenty-One

Operation Wildhorn III

Moonlight shone down and guided the three partisans as Grandpa Andrzej's cart plodded along the back-country roads. Colin lay sleeping on the bumpy potatoes with his left arm around Noah. Jozef reached from the front seat to shake him awake. "Colin, we're almost at the meeting point to rendezvous with the officers. Look sharp."

Colin climbed on the seat between Grandpa Andrzej and Jozef. "See the two men by the trees?" Andrzej said. "They're high-ranking officers in the Armia Krajowa."

"The what?" Colin asked.

"The Armia Krajowa is the official name for the Home Army," Jozef said.

"How can you tell those guys are high ranking?"

"They're the only ones with those crisp green uniforms belted at the waist. Maybe your rank as a first lieutenant is high enough to be issued one of those." Grandpa Andrzej chuckled.

As they jumped down from the wagon, Captain Batory signaled for the three to join them at a nearby grove of oak trees. Everything about the captain screamed discipline, from his always polished boots to his neatly trimmed mustache. "Welcome, Colin. I hear your codename is 'Goon.' Highly unusual."

Colin wanted to explain how a goon in ice hockey had the unofficial role of responding to any dirty or violent play by the opposition. This wasn't the time or place, so he just nodded.

"Captain, where exactly is our final destination?" Jozef inquired.

"A field in Zaborow, just twenty minutes from here. We have bikes for both you and Colin, and that's how you'll have to get home. Use your best judgment about the 'ghost on a bicycle' problem if Germans suddenly appear."

Grandpa Andrzej strode up to Colin and embraced him. "Well, I've done my part, but your blessing or magic certainly helped us during the first part of our journey. An old man and his cart of potatoes traveling in the dark would surely have given cause for an arrest. Maybe, Colin, you made us all invisible. Will we ever know?"

Colin somehow knew this was the last time he would ever again see his grandfather. Grandpa Andrzej held Colin in front of him for inspection. "Now, it's almost dawn and time for me to leave you." Tears streamed from the old man's eyes. "Someday, the winds will brush all these tyrants away, but I won't live to see that day." Andrzej placed both hands on top of his cane. "Soon, I'll be buried in the ground. Promise me when I'm gone, you'll carry on our dream of freedom and work for peace. Whatever has happened in Poland would be a thousand times more terrible if anyone repaid our wounds by inflicting new ones on others."

Colin didn't fully understand what his grandfather was saying, but they again embraced before Andrzej broke away in anguish. Colin and Jozef stood with Noah between them and watched as Andrzej's horse and cart faded into the distance.

One of the mysterious Home Army officers, who had been huddling in the forest with the unit, came to join Colin and Jozef. "Time to move on, men. We need to be at Zaborow by daybreak where we'll learn the details of the transfer. The local farmers are letting us store the cases of missile parts in their barns, but first, may I get a look at this magic phone?"

Colin removed it from his pocket and displayed it for the officer.

"Astonishing! We can't wait until we see how it's used."

Jozef smirked as the officer mounted his bicycle. "Colin, at least he didn't call it 'remarkable'!"

The early morning skies gave just enough light to guide the partisans as they pedaled to Zaborow. From a distance, they spotted a farmer sprinting from his field waving a stalk of barley in one hand

and a hoe in the other. Colin's first reaction was to panic, but the others shouted with joy and walked their bikes through the soggy field to greet him.

"Everyone else is here, except some of the other farmers who'll help with lighting up the field when it's time," the farmer said.

In the barn amidst the cows and clucking chickens were suitcases, large wooden crates, and about eight men sitting on straw bales. Batory smiled. "Good evening, our brothers! My unit had such a long ride, but ours was nothing compared to your travels all the way from Warsaw!"

The farmer mysteriously dashed to his house and soon returned carrying two prized bottles of vodka under each arm. "Brothers, let's first toast to each man here and their sacrifice for Poland. May we all be protected by God Almighty, and Poland restored to her former glory!"

"Nastrovya! We also need to salute our two invisible partisans from America! A young man and his dog!" Another toast rang out as the bottles passed from man to man.

When Colin reached out for the container, Jozef just glared, "Goon, you don't want to get sick today, do you?"

Colin pretended to be disappointed but knew he needed to keep his mind clear for this critical task.

Jozef proudly stood next to Colin. "Probably not many of you can see them, but I assure you—Colin, who is my nephew, and his fine dog, Noah, are nearby. The dog is a giant and is a well-trained sentry animal who will alert us to any disturbances. If you can't see them, you also won't hear Noah's bark. Only Captain Batory, Marek, and I—who are their blood relations—can see and hear them."

Captain Batory, perched on one of the precious cases, rose to take command of the gathering. "Men, now that everyone is here, I'll explain the mission. A fully intact V-2 missile was found near Sarnaki by a farmer who arrived at the landing site before the Germans swarmed the area. It was Colin's sister, Elise, who alerted us that the Germans were aiming the V-2s at that region. The farmer contacted his cell, and they dragged the missile to the river and buried it under reeds. When the Germans arrived, they must have been very disappointed to discover not even one shiny fragment."

Everyone's fist went up to cheer and honor these partisans, and then Captain Batory continued. "After the local unit was certain the Germans had abandoned their recovery, the partisans brought the missile by horse and wagon to this very barn. Thanks to the diagrams and instruction from the research provided by First Lieutenant Colin, we disassembled it and drew sketches before it was sent to Warsaw. The local AK disguised themselves as farmers and transported the parts by wagons along the backroads. Of course, our men shadowed the wagons and were willing to fight to the death for the success of this mission. Pity those unfortunate horses with the weight of the missile and all of those potatoes!"

Everyone laughed and then Captain Batory went on with his story. "A team of scientists broke this three-ton missile down into about 25,000 parts, and you won't believe this next part. One scientist, who studied the electronic components of the missile, worked during the day in a German officer's apartment in Warsaw. He kept many of the smallest parts in a suitcase and stored it under his bed. The German officer's chef worked with us and would call the officer each afternoon and ask what he wanted for dinner that night and when he would return home. That servant must have seemed to be the most attentive chef in all of Warsaw! The scientist would return the items to the suitcase and leave well before the officer returned home for his dinner. All done right under the stupid Nazi's nose!" The men all laughed heartily at the daring tale.

Captain Batory resumed his story. "Sitting next to these nineteen suitcases holding the missile parts and instructions is Colonel Brzechwa. He's responsible for the planning and safety of the landing site."

Brzechwa was a brusk middle-aged man with a thick mustache who always had control of his men and tolerated no less than their full compliance. "We've been waiting over two weeks for this rain to stop and for this blasted beet field to dry up so we can use it as our landing field."

Pointing to the cases, Brzechwa continued. "These hold the missile parts, reports, and photographs. We'll be adding the recent maps and diagrams Colin brought from Blizna. They'll all be smuggled to Italy and then on to London. No details about this missile have ever been seen by any scientist or army outside of Germany. That's how important our mission is!"

Chapter Twenty-Two

So Many Problems!

After spending most of the tedious day huddled in the barn listening to the radio transmissions from Warsaw, all the men were on edge. Jozef reached for his empty coffee cup and spoke into the bottom. "All I think about is my mother, Elise, and the others. Are they safe at home? Have the Germans taken my family?"

Colin threw some clean straw onto the clay ground and sat next to his uncle. "At least we know Elise is pretty safe because the Germans can't see her. Remember, the other partisans are watching over the house, and besides, the family, including your mother, all gave their oath to fight for freedom."

The piercing squeal of an incoming transmission rang through the barn, and everyone sprinted over to hear the news. Warsaw announced they could finally schedule the flight!

Old Brzechwa stared at the cigarette between his fingers. He put the short stub to his lips, sucked in his last puff, and smashed it into the ground with his boot. Brzechwa then signaled for the men to gather. "Our field must be well-lit so the English pilot can see the landing area at night. Tonight, farmers will arrive with oil lanterns covered with a cylinder made of stiff black paper. These lanterns can't be seen from the side, but the light will be visible to the pilot from above. We'll all stand in position around the perimeter of the airfield, and when I give the signal, everyone will remove the black paper. The pilot will be searching for the square outline of our illuminated field."

Brzechwa lumbered over to the suitcases and cargo destined for the plane. "Then, as soon as the plane lands, we'll transfer these suitcases and the five men onto the plane, and it'll take off. These suitcases can't get into the hands of the Germans or the Russians. This mission could be a fight to the death."

"Do you all understand this?" Batory asked. "Our goal is to stop the Germans from getting to the airfield to prevent the plane from landing or taking off. If the Germans arrive before the plane takes off, we might all be slaughtered."

Colin and Noah rested in the shade against the barn while Jozef leaned against the tattered barn door. They scanned the landscape, with one eye on the road and the other on the forest's edge, when Noah suddenly let out a stream of alarming barks. "Uncle Jozef, look over there—two of our men are running from the woods to the barn. They're waving for everyone to gather."

After identifying themselves to the leaders, the men turned to all the partisans. "Another problem! Three German planes landed on our airfield just a few hours ago, and the pilots left them there. We passed the news to Warsaw. They suggested we use horses to drag the planes off the airfield. We've done reconnaissance in the area, and the Germans now have a watch all around that field. There's no way we can just drag the planes off with horses!"

"Are they crazy? The Germans would slaughter every one of us!" Brzechwa sprang up from a stool with his arms flailing while letting out a litany of profanities.

Jozef felt the pulse beating in his throat with his clammy hands. "First the rain and soaked fields with German troops a mile away, and now three Storches on the field. What next?"

The full moon cast an encouraging light early that evening when a roar thundered in the distant skies. Colin sprang to his feet and ran out the door and saw the Storches flying away from the area. The Germans still had no clue of the Home Army's presence on the nearby farm and also removed their guards from the field. Even the brusque Brzechwa bellowed out a cheer for this good news. The mission could finally commence!

July 25th hosted a clear, pitch-dark night as Jozef, Colin, and the other partisans readied to take their positions on the field. Brzechwa gathered them for their final orders. "Now we wait. Remember, the Germans are just a mile away." His forehead furrowed as he pointed to each man. "I swear, I'll shoot anyone who lights a cigarette." Colin didn't doubt Brzechwa would carry through on that threat. At that moment, Colin swore he would never take up the deadly habit.

Brzechwa continued. "At the sound of my whistle, everyone on the landing field will remove the cardboard sleeve from the lantern. When the aircraft lands, extinguish the lanterns and hurry to put the cases on the plane. When the plane leaves, scatter into the woods and make your way back home."

Jozef and Colin sat hunched, clinging to their lanterns on the carefully plotted field for over an hour waiting for the signal. Suddenly, the sound of engines wailing like the devil abruptly shattered the still night air. A faint light signal blinked—the plane was about to arrive!

Brzechwa's whistle alerted the team to remove the covers. Colin lifted the black paper from both of his lanterns and was awestruck with the sight of the twinkling airfield.

But instead of landing, the plane's engines screamed and continued back into the air. After a few minutes, Colin saw the plane circling for another landing. He was sure the Germans were alerted to the plane's presence and worried they might swarm upon the field at any moment.

Colin's heart was in his throat when the Dakota finally touched down. He waited until the doors opened and hurried to help Jozef load two suitcases onto the airplane. The small guard of local AK partisans whisked four mysterious passengers off the plane, and they disappeared into the forests.

Five partisans boarded within minutes, and everything proceeded like clockwork. The crew fastened the door while the pilot attempted to start the engines, but there was silence. After several more tries, the engines finally started and the Dakota moved a short distance, but then wouldn't budge.

The exasperated pilot opened the door and shouted down to Jozef, "The brakes have probably locked up! There doesn't seem to be anything we can do to get this plane moving!"

Jozef turned to the pilot and shouted, "There has to be *something* we can do!"

Clearly aggravated, the pilot glared back at them to deliver the crew's decision. "No, we don't have time. Remove the suitcases. We have to torch this plane!"

"Not on my watch!" yelled Batory. Jozef and Colin climbed onto the plane and began inspecting the inside.

Jozef bellowed, "Do you understand there are other risks if you burn this plane? The Nazis will kill all the locals in the nearby village in revenge. Do you want to risk all the innocent villagers who'll be killed? Let's at least take out your guns and rifles to defend ourselves."

The pilot shot back at him, "What guns? We had to leave them behind to make space for fuel. The missile parts alone weigh tons!"

Colin's mind was ablaze with confusion. "Uncle Jozef, the English didn't say anything about all these problems in their histories I read. They said nothing about setting the plane on fire. There has to be a solution!"

Colin whipped out his cell phone and pressed the *on* button. "Maybe Grandma wrote about it." He keyed in her website and followed the link to "WWII history in Poland." There it was: Operation Wildhorn III! Colin frantically read the details and yelled, "Got it! I know what the problem is. The front tires are stuck in the mud!"

Colin jumped out of the plane and shined the cell phone's light onto the submerged tire. "Look, just like grandma's story reported! She said you guys pushed wooden sideboards from the carts under the tires and then built a short runway with old doors and anything hard and flat to build a short runway."

Colin's discovery energized all the partisans who dashed around the farm looking for boards, large stones, and planks. Jozef rushed up to the pilot after he assessed the makeshift runway. "Keep it straight as an arrow. There'll be enough surface for you to lift off."

The pilot commended Jozef with a hearty handshake. "Never saw anything like this team of partisans. Remarkable!"

With the crew and suitcases all back on the plane, the engines fired up, and the aircraft crept forward to see if the planks would hold. The plane then roared down the runway and ascended into the nighttime skies.

"That pilot didn't even know I was here, did he?" Colin asked.

"I'm afraid not, but everyone down here on the ground knows."

Jozef and Colin lingered only until the plane was no longer visible.

Colin breathed a sigh of relief. "Mission accomplished. Come on, Noah, let's get out of here!" His heart beat with confidence and pride. All the partisans fled into the woods with their bicycles, amazed that no Germans had spotted the operation.

Colin and Jozef mounted their bikes and with Noah at their side, pedaled furiously back to their home in Niwiska.

Chapter Twenty-Three

Back home

Adam and Elise sat on the back steps throwing pebbles in a circle they had made with their fingers in the sandy soil. "Colin just isn't himself since he and Uncle Jozef returned home," said Adam.

Elise replied, "He should be happy, like Uncle Jozef. He said the mission went well and that Colin is a big hero."

Adam slumped forward. "Boy, I wish I could have been there."

Elise jumped to her feet. "Maybe Colin needs some company." She skipped to the front yard to find Colin cuddling with Noah. "How are the two big war heroes?"

Colin reacted only by lifting his shoulders up and down. Elise had never seen Colin this upset before, so she sat next to him. "What's wrong, Colin? Was it like a scary movie?"

"Not really. I knew by reading the history on the English website that the mission was going to be successful, but then I read more of Grandma's website. Things are going to get scary right here in Niwiska really soon. People are going to get arrested sometime this week or next. Grandma didn't give dates. Some people are going to be sent to a concentration camp. I just read Father Kurek was among the arrested."

"Father Kurek! We have to warn him! Does Grandma mention the others so we can also warn them?"

"Elise, I have only three-percent charge left. I had to power off." Colin stretched his eyes to prevent tears from forming. "Things aren't going to end well here either. After the Germans leave, the Russians will take over."

"Not the Americans?" Elise asked.

"No, they're hundreds of miles away. Russia will have complete control over this region." Colin's voice choked. "Really, over all of Poland. The people here are going from one evil ruler to another. The only good thing is that because of our mission, London will be saved from the worst of the missile attacks, but the English will take all the credit. Grandma's article said so. After all, it was their pilot and their plane who brought back the V-2 parts."

Elise leaped to her feet. "Colin, we have to warn Father Kurek that he's in danger. No one is home besides Adam, so you and I have to find him."

"Adam and I will go to where the unit camped last night, but you walk toward the manor close to the tree lines and see if Father Kurek's on his bike somewhere nearby. Take Noah with you."

Colin hugged his little sister and then darted off into the forests leading to Blizna.

Elise stood to put her arms around her dog. "We need to think about how you can help." He nuzzled close to her with his snout. "That's it! You're such a smart dog. Stay! Stay right here!"

Noah sat obediently while Elise flew into and then immediately back out of the house. "Father Kurek gave me this pretty necklace that was his mother's. It should have his scent on it."

She knelt in front of Noah, held the necklace in her palm, and placed it by Noah's nose. "Find Father Kurek." She then hung it around his massive furry neck. "You can do it! Find Father Kurek and bring him to me."

Elise opened the front gate, and as if he fully understood his assignment, Noah bounded down the road. He then came to a screeching halt and sniffed near a row of weeds and ran at a breakneck pace to the north.

As Noah's figure became just a speck and out of her view, Elise stood perplexed. *Now, what should I do? Stay? Go in the woods to try to find him? I have to do something!*

Elise raced back to the house and put a rope around Leia's collar. "Leia, I need you with me because this is really scary!" The two began their search in the direction of Grandpa Andrzej's home. Although she had never been there, Elise had seen him come down this road when he visited. *Perhaps Father Kurek is making visits to his parishioners.*

Elise's heart raced wildly. She wandered from tree to tree with her head tilted upward to scan the faces of the trees. Every few steps, she stopped and surveyed to the right and left, but soon only saw trees that all resembled one another. Thoughts of her parents, of Colin, and her predictable, safe neighborhood flooded her mind.

From a distance, the angry thunder from two German trucks rolling under Niwiska's peaceful skies intensified. As they moved closer, Elise and Leia instinctively ran farther into the forest. Positioned safely behind a large tree, Elise heard screams from the truck as it drove past and saw several people waving their arms in protest. *Were these villagers just arrested and was Father Kurek amongst them?*

The trucks whisked by too quickly for Elise to discern if the passengers were young or old, men or women. It was all a blur, and she sat on the ground and sobbed. Leia gently jumped up and licked her cheek. "You're right, Leia, we have just one option—to continue our search for Father Kurek." With each stride, her mind became more resolute. Elise realized she was in charge of the priest's destiny. His safety lay squarely in her own hands—and Leia's.

Elise broke into a trot and continued to hug the tree line, but stopped at regular points to survey in all directions. When she finally arrived at the fork in the road, another decision had to be made. *Should I head toward the manor house to tell Maria and Jadwiga about Father Kurek, or should I continue down the road leading to the town of Kolbuszowa where he sometimes stays at their priest's house?*

It then occurred to Elise why the Nazis chose this heavily forested area for their training camp. Camp Heidelager was truly a wilderness where they could hide their top-secret projects out of view from most people.

Leia began to tug on the rope in the direction of the manor house, so they both sprinted down that open road.

All of a sudden, Leia came to a screeching halt and began to bark at something on the other road. Elise then saw a fleck of white and brown. After just a few seconds, she saw Noah run at full gallop with

Father Kurek cycling behind, his cape fluttering in the wind. She pivoted and ran toward them and hugged them both.

"You weren't on that truck!" Elise embraced the priest while Leia jumped up on him. "Oh, Father Kurek, Colin read on my grandma's website that the Germans want to arrest you. We have to get you to safety so they can't find you!"

The priest's eyes bulged out, and he clutched his hands to his heaving chest. "Someone must have been tortured and gave my name as a partisan." He weaved in all directions as he considered what his next move would be.

"Why don't you hide up in the church's roof? I can see it right outside our window, and there's never any Germans nearby."

"There's a door in the back room that leads up to it. I'll hide there until the danger of my arrest is over. The Germans are getting ready to leave, so it shouldn't be too long. That's why there are so many trucks heading west toward Germany."

"We need to get out of here quick. I just saw two trucks heading west!" Elise yelled.

"Hop on the back, and I'll give you a ride back home."

Father Kurek and Elise raced home with both dogs padding beside his bike, and when they arrived, Colin and Adam were standing at the gate.

"No time to explain, but Adam, I need for you to take this bike to the partisans. Only tell them I'm safe but not where I'm going. It isn't safe for anyone to know if the Nazis get ahold of them."

The priest embraced Elise. "Lord Hupka told us you and Colin were here to save at least one life. Maybe my life is the one you will save."

Father Kurek bent down to pet Noah. "You, Mr. Noah, you and Elise saved my life."

Elise picked up Leia and squeezed her tight. "It was Leia who heard you and Noah on another road. She stopped me from going down the wrong road. Leia's a hero too!"

Father Kurek kissed both dogs on top of their heads. "Elise, tell only Jadwiga where I'm going. She'll know what to do." He then ran in the direction of the church cemetery.

Adam, Colin, and Elise took turns guarding the windows, waiting for the first sign of Maria, Jadwiga, or Jozef. Colin walked over to his sister and put his hands on his hips. "Come on, Elise. You can tell me where Father Kurek is hiding."

Adam sat at the table and stirred his soup. "Quit badgering her, Colin. She's right. The fewer people who know, the better. Remember what we just heard from Uncle Jozef about Henryk and his family? They might have been those people Elise saw in the truck. Someone probably snitched to the Germans about Henryk and Father Kurek's last mission."

"What if the Germans find Father Kurek? Then what?" Colin asked.

Adam rested his fist against his cheek and stared in his empty bowl in front of him. "*Then what?* Then he dies! If it's his time, and he dies for a righteous cause, that is one thing. Dying to end your own misery, like my grandfather and Uncle Roman did, is something else." Adam looked as if he was ready to cry.

The three sat silently while Colin cradled his slowly dying phone.

"You must really miss your Uncle Roman," Colin said.

"The only thing I remember about Uncle Roman was him sitting over in that chair and staring into the fireplace. The flames would crackle and flicker, and Uncle Roman would sit for hours in a trance."

Adam slid down the wooden bench closer to Colin. "What about you? I bet you miss your house and all those fantastic games and toys. Playing soccer and those other games with sticks."

Colin had a wistful look on his face. "I almost never think about those things anymore. They don't seem all that important. What I really miss is my mom and dad, my grandparents and my friends, my neighbors, and even my teachers."

Elise chimed in. "Me too. It's weird, in a certain way. I love my family here and helping the partisans, but I miss sitting on my mom's lap and watching TV and my dad coaching my softball team. I think about Papa taking us to find fossils and Grandma teaching me to cook and sew. I used to be really afraid of sleeping away from home. Look at me now!"

Colin stared at his cell phone. "When we first got here, I thought this adventure would be over in a day and 'poof,' we'd be back home. Now I wonder if we'll be here forever."

Chapter Twenty-Four

Elise to the Rescue

A steady flow of trucks flew down the roads, all heading west in the direction of Germany. Most were loaded with soldiers, but a few only carried furniture and large paintings. Through the windows from inside the house, the children saw Maria holding Jadwiga by the arm as they walked on the grassy areas to avoid the madness.

As soon as they rushed through the gate, Jadwiga collapsed on the bench in front of the house. "Water, I need water," she panted.

"It's madness at the manor house! Heiss and the others are preparing to leave and have taken absolutely anything of value." Maria's chest heaved up and down as she tried to catch her breath. "There'll be nothing there tomorrow, including any German officers."

"Babcia! Maria! The Germans are arresting people, and they're looking for Father Kurek!" yelled Elise as she ran to embrace the women.

Colin rushed from the house with a cup of water for both women. "Father Kurek was just here, but he's gone into hiding. Only Elise knows where he is."

"He said to tell only Babcia." Elise's voice trailed off as she whispered the secret into Jadwiga's ear.

Colin asked, "Now what should we do?"

"Colin, you go with Elise to take supplies to Father Kurek. No German can do anything to you, so you'll be safe… but bring the dogs. They'll alert you to any Germans who might be pursuing him," Jadwiga said.

Maria said, "The soldiers have taken dozens from the village as prisoners to the train station. Most villagers are hiding in shelters in the fields near the Wisloka River. Adam and I will join them there and bring our cow and some hens. German soldiers are stealing everyone's livestock."

Jadwiga walked toward the front door. "I need to rest for a while before I make that long journey. Colin and Elise will help with the other cart. I'll pack it with blankets and food."

Jadwiga scurried through the kitchen, collecting food and a blanket for Father Kurek. She placed all the food in Noah's saddlebags and put the rest of the items in pails for Elise and Colin to carry. "The lock on the side door of the church is broken. Go in and walk to the altar and then turn to the left. The room there has a small door in the ceiling. Find a stick to tap at the door and call out for him."

Elise nodded and scampered to her bed to grab her doll. "I'm going to let Father Kurek have Eva to keep him company."

Jadwiga embraced them both. "Eva will stay much cleaner up there, and Father Kurek will think of you all the time if she is with him."

The children and dogs stood at the door to see if any German trucks were in view. Assured they were in the clear, the four dashed across the road. As they ran across the fields in the direction of the church, Colin looked behind him to see only Leia following him. She jumped up and down and kept pivoting to tell him something. "Where's Noah? Elise, Noah isn't with us!"

"Leia's trying to tell us something!" Elise said. The corgi's pathetic howl signaled them to turn around.

"Leia, do you know where Noah is?" Colin asked. Leia dashed back a few feet, trotted about the ground, and guided the children to Noah.

There, near a tree, Noah's right front leg was caught in a mass of tangled thorns. "Noah, what happened?" Elise cried.

"Look, his leg's cut up by the thorns. Elise, give me that towel in the pail, and I'll wrap it around the thorny branch."

Leia distracted Noah by licking him all over his face while Colin deftly removed his leg from the web of thorns.

Elise buried her head into Noah's quivering body. "Don't worry, Noah. I'm a Girl Guide, and we know how to perform first aid. I'll get some water from the well by the church to clean your wounds." Elise hurriedly drew water from the well and bathed Noah's gashes as best she could.

"We need to get to the church, Elise. It's right up this path."

As they entered, both children flinched when the door's creak echoed throughout the abandoned building with no windows. Dried, crinkly leaves scattered on the floor crunched as they walked up to the altar and then to the left. Just as Jadwiga had described, there was a wooden door in the ceiling.

Colin found a cane-like stick sitting near a large shelf. He jumped on a counter to reach the door and tapped on it and bellowed, "It's Colin and Elise!"

The door slowly opened, and the children saw Father Kurek's beaming face.

"Children!" The priest lowered a wooden ladder from his rooftop room. "You came so quickly!"

Elise said, "We had to because we need to join the villagers hiding from the Germans near the river. Here's some food for you, some blankets, pails, and things Jadwiga thinks you'll need."

"So, Jadwiga knows?"

"Yes, she's the one who gathered all this up and is at home preparing to leave," Colin said.

Colin and Elise scampered up the ladder to bring the supplies up for the priest.

Elise sat on her knees and inspected the massive timber roof area and boxes scattered about. "What's in these boxes?"

"Just candles and books. I've been preparing this place for a few weeks just in case someone needed to hide out. Looks like it ended up being me." Father Kurek pointed to several sleeping sacks and jugs. "I even brought up water."

"We need to be going to help Jadwiga over to the river," Elise said.

They all climbed down the ladder, and Father Kurek sat on the ground to let the dogs cuddle with him. "Noah, what happened to your leg?"

"He got his leg tangled in thorns," Elise reported.

"There are some old bandages in this drawer. Let's get that bleeding stopped."

After Elise wrapped the bandage around Noah's leg, the children stood to leave.

"Well, Father Kurek, you'll be good for a week or so," Colin said. "I guess I'll see you then."

"No, Colin, I don't suspect you will. Something tells me you'll both be gone by that time."

"I wish my cell phone could better tell the future. It has only about ten more minutes of research left. I might as well turn it on to see if Grandma's stories tell me any more history."

Colin and Elise sat next to Father Kurek as the cell phone powered up. "Just two-percent left. So far, Grandma's website has the best information about WWII in Niwiska. Let's see…"

Colin's eyes scanned an article he had never seen before. "Hey, here's a part about you, Father Kurek! *'Father Jan Kurek, the priest from St. Nicholas in Niwiska, was a committed and exemplary priest and patriot. He was a chaplain for the local Home Army and together with Henryk Augustyn, played an instrumental role in the decoding of information found on bits of shrapnel and rockets. This activity helped the Allies learn how to dismantle unexploded Nazi shells. They were arrested and sent to Sachsenhausen Concentration Camp.'* That's all it says."

Father Kurek gasped and his entire body tensed. "Henryk and his entire family were arrested, but I obviously escaped. Do you think this report is wrong?"

Colin noted the alarm in the priest's eyes. "Maybe this story is only talking about Henryk and his family being arrested," Colin muttered. "Here's a link to our family tree. It shows that Jadwiga lived to about the age of ninety-five, and Maria also lived a long time.

Here's extra information about Adam. It says he had a son named Michael who became a priest right here in Niwiska!"

Colin's face then became somber. "But Michael drowned in 1999, and Adam was so depressed he took his own life right after that."

"Not Adam!" Elise clutched her doll. "Look for Uncle Jozef. Did he get married and have children after the war?"

"It says he got married in 1945 and had four children, so things must have turned out okay. Here's a story about him. It's called 'Jozef Batory and Jozef Bryk: Two Cursed Soldiers.' Captain Batory's in the story too!"

"Look, Grandma actually knew about Uncle Jozef, and that he was a soldier. Maybe he became as important as Captain Batory!" Elise said.

Colin looked puzzled. "What's a cursed soldier?"

Without warning, all five startled at a peculiar whistling, roaring sound from the outside that rattled the foundations of the church building. Then, like the grand finale of Fourth of July fireworks, the canon-like sounds intensified. Colin and Elise ran to the front of the church in the direction of the commotion. They spotted blinding flashes from the west, and then more explosions as a tremendous white cloud rose in the air.

I don't remember any mention of this in any of Grandma's stories! Maybe the Germans are blowing up all the missiles before they run off, so they don't leave any evidence." Colin frantically tried to search with keywords to find a reference but noted the phone was flashing. It was about to shut down.

Colin, Elise, and the dogs huddled at the top of the church steps.

Elise covered her eyes as Leia burrowed into her arms. "This looks like the end of the world, Colin!"

Noah stood in front of the children as if he was trying to protect them from the horrifying sight of exploding V-1 and V-2 missiles. Then, silence blanketed the air, and the intense vibrations ended. Silence.

Figure 3 Door to Father Kurek's hiding place in the church

Figure 4 Father Jan Kurek

Chapter Twenty-Five

Finally Back Home

Silence still permeated the air. Colin was the first to open his eyes. He lifted his arm from around his sister's trembling shoulders. "Elise?"

"Colin? Noah? Leia? You're all here!" Elise stood and surveyed the dimly lit room. "This is our family room! We're back in our family room!"

Colin rose from the smooth wooden floor and circled all around. There on the side table was the gromnica, slightly smoldering. He shook his head and glanced around the room as if looking for answers. "This is going to sound silly, but I had a dream we were somewhere else."

Elise's eyes were like saucers. "Me too, but it couldn't have been!"

"I think it did happen. Look at the doll you're holding!"

"It's Eva! The doll Jozef gave me! I was going to give it to Father Kurek."

"Oh, this is too weird. We might have both had the same dream." Colin wrinkled his eyebrows. "Were you in Poland?"

"I think I was, and the dogs were there too!" Elise exclaimed. "Oh, I wish you two could talk so we could figure this out." Leia jumped up on Colin's legs, but Noah tried to nuzzle up to him. "Look at the bandage on his leg! He got cut up in thorns on the way to the church!"

"So, Colin, do you remember any of the people like Jozef, Jadwiga, Adam, and Maria?"

Colin flopped onto the couch, "And Father Kurek, and Grandpa Andrzej, and the partisans?"

"So, we weren't dreaming, Colin. Somehow, we traveled back in time to World War II! Is that what you remember?"

At that moment, headlights beamed as a car entered the driveway, and within a minute, their parents flew through the front door.

Greg called out, "We're home! A tree fell down right in front of us and blocked our way for over an hour."

"Are you two okay?" Jessica ran to hug them. "The local cell phone towers are down, and we couldn't get through to you. I kept trying to call."

"Ugh, the lights are out all over the neighborhood, but at least the storm has finally blown out of the area." Greg found a powerful LED lantern in the cabinet and set it on the table next to the gromnica. "Did you guys light this candle?"

With the brighter light illuminating the room, their mother gasped at her two children. "Wow, you two need a serious shower, and Colin, tomorrow I'll take you for a haircut. How did it get so shaggy in just one day?"

Greg sat on the floor to examine Noah's leg. "Jess, when did Noah hurt his leg? I took him for a run before dinner and didn't see this bandage." He unwrapped the bandage to further examine Noah's injury. "This is a fresh wound."

Jessica took a slight step back and scanned the children and dogs from head to toe. "What's been going on guys? I thought I could trust you for the two hours we were gone."

Colin put his arm around Elise, who seemed ready to cry. "You aren't going to believe this. *We* can't even believe what just happened!"

Elise hugged Eva and then bounced up and down. "Mom, look at this doll. Uncle Jozef gave it to me. It was Valerie's before she died."

"Elise, who is this Jozef who gave you that ragged old doll?" her father asked.

Elise's eyes lit up. "Colin, this is proof! Eva came back with us! I was holding her when the missiles were exploding. I meant to give it to Father Kurek!"

"Elise! Jadwiga is at the house all by herself waiting for us!" Colin screamed. "She'll never make it to the river without our help!"

"Hey, guys, you're acting really weird. When we left, you two were doing your homework and getting ready for bed." Jessica began to tear up. "This is all scaring me!"

Greg held up his hands to calm his family. "Let's all sit down on the couches and hear your stories."

While he was walking over to join his parents, Colin reached into his pockets. "My cell phone! Look—all the power has been drained!"

Both dogs came to the carpet, and instead of jumping up to demand attention, they sat as still as rocks side by side. Greg's eyes shifted from dog to dog. "What's gotten into these two? They're not their usual maniac selves."

"Mom and Dad, you're not going to believe this, but we went back in time to the Second World War in Poland and helped the partisans fight the Nazis. I even got to participate in delivering a V-2 to the English!"

"Yeah, Colin's an honorary first lieutenant in the Home Army, and I'm an honorary second lieutenant AND an official Girl Guide, like Cousin Anna!" Elise pointed to her silver pin and cloth Girl Guide's badge. "Colin has a pin too!"

Colin and Elise began their story while their parents sat dumbfounded for about five minutes. "Wait, I hate for you guys to start all over, but I want Grandma and Papa to hear this," said Jessica. "The things you're talking about sound like all their jibber-jabber about Poland."

Jessica kept shaking her head in disbelief as she called her parents. "Mom, get Dad on the speakerphone. Colin and Elise have a story they insist is true, and maybe it'll make sense to you. Okay, you two, start at the beginning with the storm."

Colin and Elise took turns telling of their adventures for at least forty-five minutes.

Colin took another sip of water. "And then we saw what looked like a war in the sky. The entire church was shaking, and then all of a sudden, we were back home."

Grandma's voice quivered. "Chills are going up and down my spine. You two seem to know more about the war and Niwiska than I do! The only part that seems incorrect is about the priest in hiding."

"That's where our time ended," Colin replied.

"I know his story pretty well because he was arrested with Henryk Augustyn. They spent a year in prison, but Henryk was released after the war ended. Father Kurek died on a death march to Germany. I'm sure of it since I've read and written several historical articles about this story. His parishioners thought he was a sensational guy."

Jessica moved closer to the phone, "Mom, there are some things here that we can't explain. Greg just looked at a wound on Noah. It was all bandaged up, and he said it looked like it could have been caused by something sharp. Colin said he got his leg cut by thorns."

Greg interjected, "Elise is holding a raggy doll she said was given to her by your relatives. She didn't have it before."

"The kids said it all began when they lit that gromnica about two hours ago. Are we all in some kind of weird dream together?" Jessica asked.

"I don't care that it's already dark outside; Dad and I are coming over right now!" Grandma exclaimed.

When Colin and Elise's grandparents arrived, the Andersons were gathered around the family history books Grandma had published.

"Hey, guys, it's getting weirder. On our drive over here, I went back to all my research about that priest. The books now indicate he lived until several years after the war, and get this: there's a whole new part in my novel about what happened and even *weirder*—it's in a different font than the rest of the book!"

"Do you mean in your published novel? I have three copies. Let me check." Jessica dashed to the den to bring out her mother's historical novel about WWII in Poland. "What page?"

"Three hundred twenty-one."

"Mine looks different too, and that part in my book is *also* in bold print!"

"No publisher would let that kind of mistake be published. This story is now all different. It says that Father Kurek hid in a space in the roof of the abandoned church for almost six months, and it was Jadwiga who secretly brought him food!"

Colin paged through the family photo book. "There's Babcia in this picture! That's her in front of their house. And that's Uncle Jozef, probably when he was older with kids."

"I called my grandmother Babcia too. Do you know her real name?" Grandma asked.

"Jadwiga. My cell phone showed that she lived to be ninety-five. That's when the battery wore out."

"Let's see that cell phone, Colin. Did you take any pictures?"

"Just one. I had to save the battery to do research for the Home Army and Allies." Colin plugged in his phone and within a minute, pulled up the photo. "Here it is. These are the men from my unit."

"They're posing for the photo. Can you point out who they are?" Papa asked.

"The one with the rifle at his side is Uncle Jozef, then Alex, Marek, Peter, and the one kneeling is Skory."

"For sure, that guy with the rifle was Jozef. Looks just like the photo in the family book." Grandma started to tear up. "There's an incredibly sad story his daughter Maria told me. After the war, Jozef continued to fight with the partisans who became known as 'cursed soldiers.' The Russians considered them to be the enemy and arrested and executed them. Jozef was about to be arrested, and that meant his entire family would also be killed. He took his own life to save theirs. He died in 1955."

"But, that's like ten years after WWII ended!" Greg said.

"Yes, but the Russians kept pursuing these men and women until about 1963. Jozef gave up his life so his wife and four children wouldn't be arrested. The Russians would also have confiscated his house and property."

Everyone sat silently for a while, considering Jozef's bravery and fate.

"A Polish genealogist sent me his death record. The cause of death was translated as 'involuntary suicide.' The priest who recorded his death obviously knew Jozef's situation and that he sacrificed his life for his family."

Jessica dabbed the tears in her eyes and hugged her two children sitting next to her. "So Colin and Elise, you saved the life of this Polish priest named Father Kurek. It looks like you rescued one person from the Nazis!"

Elise leaned over to Colin, "If we saved at least one life this time, that means we can save Uncle Jozef!"

"If we light the gromnica again, will it send us back to Poland where we left off or to 1955?" Colin was bursting with excitement. "What if we try to go back to *before* 1939 and stop the Germans from invading Poland? Then, the Second World War would never have happened!"

Everyone stared at the candle, not knowing what the next step should be.

"This may sound harsh, but I don't think you two should tell anyone else about this story. I totally believe you, because there are so many unexplained details. I'm convinced you didn't make this up," Greg said.

Papa shook his head in agreement. "Something amazing happened in the past few hours, but other people, especially reporters, will think you made all this up, maybe even with our help just for the publicity."

"I'm still having a hard time believing this ever happened. All I know is that Elise and I need to find some way to go back and save Uncle Jozef!" Colin said.

"Colin and Elise, perhaps you might never be able to return where you left off, but maybe you two are meant to help others with this magical candle," Grandma said.

Elise grinned, "You mean, Colin, Elise, *AND* Leia and Noah!"

Afterword

The Young Partisans is a unique novel as it is both fantasy and time travel mixed with serious history. Of course, Colin and Elise weren't actually in Poland during World War II, but their ancestors were! All the main characters were real people who lived through these frightening experiences, and most of the problems and history presented in the story were real. Jozef, Anna and Father Kurek were Home Army partisans fighting the war against the Nazis, and Jadwiga, Maria, Adam, Andrzej, and Lord Hupka were their family and neighbors.

What became of the real people from *The Young Partisans?*

After the Second World War, the village of Niwiska sat behind the Iron Curtain under Russian control until Poland won its freedom in 1989. The post-war years were extremely difficult for everyone in Poland, especially those who were partisans like Jozef, Anna, and Father Kurek who served in the Home Army, also known as the Armia Krajowa (AK). The Russians perceived them as enemies, and their soldiers became known as the "Cursed" or "Doomed" Soldiers who were arrested, tried in sham military trials, and then executed.

Slowly, Poland began to rebuild under a communist regime, but the people continued to live in extreme poverty. Many Polish Americans sent financial and material support to their families.

Functional wooden and concrete homes were built in Niwiska and the surrounding villages after the 1960s, yet many still lived in old wooden homes with clay floors and tin or thatched roofs until the later part of the 1980s.

The Hupka Manor House was left in poor condition by the Russians but was restored when Poland became part of the European Union. It serves as a community center and library. There is a modern and respected school of music in the old servants' quarters.

Today, there is little evidence of the wartime experiences in Niwiska and the surrounding area. The homes are charming, the church has been restored, and a few stores are servicing the locals. If you know where to look, you will find museums and places that are preserved to tell the shocking story of Camp Heidelager. Blizna Historical Park is dedicated to keeping alive the story of Hitler's top-secret V-1 and V-2 missile research facility. There is also a museum at the site of the Pustkow Concentration Camp.

Anna Grabiec went on to begin her training as a teacher after the war. She returned to Niwiska and taught in its local schools for many years. Anna married a man who had the same name as her father (Wladyslaw or Walter Grabiec) and so retained her maiden name. She had two children, Antoni and Maria.

Anna's greatest legacy has been the numerous letters she wrote to tell the history of WWII in Poland. These letters were the inspiration for this novel and the source for many of its true stories. Anna died in 2012.

Jozef Bryk married on June 1944, shortly before the Germans were pushed out by the Russians. Jozef's life as a partisan is told in an article written for **www.Doomed Soldiers.com** in Poland. His death certificate states that he died of "involuntary suicide" in 1955 and was buried in the church cemetery.

Jadwiga Bryk remained in her home across the road from St. Nicholas Church until her death in 1962. Jadwiga lived until age 95 and her grandchildren's memories, especially of her helping Father Kurek while he was hiding in the church, tell of her remarkable character and tenacity. Jadwiga is the author's great-grandmother.

Maria Bryk continued to live in the family home until her death in 1995. She worked as the priests' cook and housekeeper. Her son, **Adam**, built a new house on the land where the one portrayed in the story once stood and raised his family.

Andrzej Cudecki was the mayor of Trzesn before the war and a farmer. He died just after the war in 1945 and is buried with his wife Jozefa (Zeffie) in Radomysl, Poland.

Father Jan Kurek has been held in high esteem in his parish's history because of his work as an exemplary priest and an AK partisan. The story of his work with the Home Army is absolutely true. When the author visited Niwiska in 2016, a parish priest showed her the access door in the sacristy to his roof hideout. Much of his story is based on the historical records he wrote after the war. Father Kurek continued to serve his parish until 1947 and died in 1971.

Captain Jozef Batory, whose AK codenames were Argus and Wojtek, was the head of the Home Army in Kolbuszowa. His tragic arrest, imprisonment, and execution story was told to the author by Frank Batory, Jozef's young brother. The article is on the author's website. His remains were never located. Today, a monument to his bravery and sacri

Dr. Jan Ernest Hupka's life ended in poverty, and he was partially paralyzed and blind. He died in Kolbuszowa in 1952 and is buried in the Hupka Chapel, located in the St. Nicholas Cemetery in Niwiska.

Dr. Hupka was a generous benefactor to the church and was a primary employer of many of the locals.

Hitler's V-1 and V-2 Missile Program:
Its Role in America's Space Program

Blizna and Niwiska share a prominent place in America's history of space travel. It was there the German's top-secret V-1 and V-2 rockets were launched for experimental and training purposes during WWII from 1943 to the summer of 1944. The research and knowledge acquired from the V-1 and V-2 missile program that ended in Blizna would lead to the first intercontinental ballistic missile, the first spy satellite, and the "small step" taken by astronaut Neil Armstrong.

V-2 missile crashing during WWII

The post-WWII space race between the Soviet Union and the United States had its origins in these remote villages because of what their scientists had learned about rocket engineering. During the war, much of this information was smuggled to the Allies due to the amazing dedication of the local foresters and AK or Armia Krajowa. The Russians pushed out the Germans in August 1944 and were desperate to retrieve missile fragments and information the Nazis had left behind.

Fragments of missile assembly area in Blizna

The story begins in the years preceding WWII. Wernher von Braun, a preeminent scientist of Germany's pre-war rocket development program and later the post-war director of NASA's Marshall Space Flight Center was inspired in the 1930s by a science fiction movie "Woman in the Moon." What had been conceived as a creative and ambitious vision of von Braun and his peers for space travel was turned into a sinister weapon of mass destruction by the Nazis. Von Braun worked at the Peenemunde and Blizna test sites and personally visited the missile impact areas to troubleshoot any problems discovered during trials.

von Braun (left, in suit) with German officers in Blizna

The development of the V-1 flying bomb and the V-2 missile was originally housed in Peenemunde on the Baltic coast in Germany until the Allies destroyed much of the facility in August 1943. While the scientists' housing was the first target, the British unfortunately also destroyed the nearby concentration camp. Some of the prisoners who perished were the ones who first alerted the British to the existence of Hitler's top-secret weapon's program.

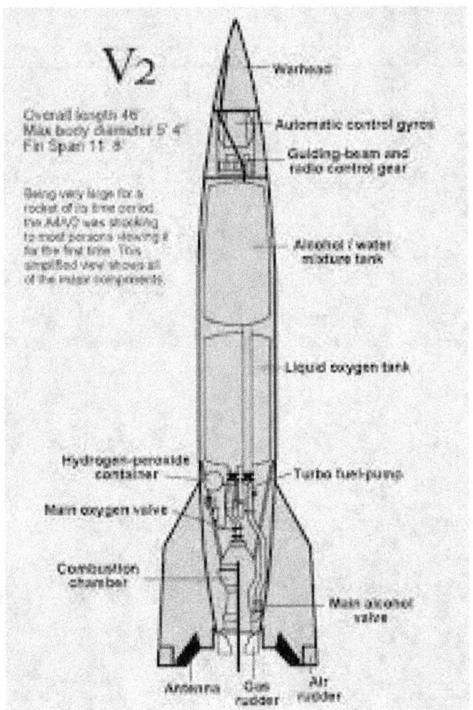

The research and testing program for the V-1 and V-2 missiles was then moved to the secluded area near Blizna in the fall of 1943. The adjacent villages of Niwiska and Pustkow had been previously evacuated to house an SS military base in the early years of the war and had been well developed by the time of the missile program's move to Blizna. Himmler himself recommended the move to this area.

The new location in Blizna was desirable as it was outside the range of the Allied bombers. Most of the villagers had already been evacuated to live in nearby villages. Other villagers who were forced to serve the Nazi's goals lived in facilities within the boundaries of Camp Heidelager, the largest SS training camp outside of Germany while they worked in construction, farming, carpentry, and as maids, cooks, and servants.

Polish Slave Laborers working for the Germans

Efforts were made to disguise the launching sites as much as possible. The Nazis built an artificial village, hoping the area would appear inhabited when the Allies took aerial photos. Cottages and barns made of plywood, lines hung with clothes and bedsheets, and plaster statues of people and animals were created to enhance the deception.

The site in Blizna was of high strategic importance and attracted personal visits from the most high-ranking Nazi officers: Heinrich Himmler, Hans Hammler, and Gottlob Berger. Adolf Hitler visited in the spring of 1944.

Himmler's visit to Blizna

The missile testing ground at Blizna, commanded by Dr. Walter Dornberger, was soon identified by the Polish resistance movement thanks to reports from local farmers and foresters. The AK field agents managed to obtain pieces of the fired rockets by arriving on the scene before German patrols. The Germans were aware of the AK, but the AK was always watching the Germans.

Polish Underground Fighters (Armia Krajowa- AK)

The AK Home Army partisans were actively involved in the sabotage of the missiles originally built at the Mittelbau-Dora Concentration Camp. A group from the Polish underground had infiltrated the crew and sabotaged the construction. Once the flawed rockets were placed on their launching pads, they did not follow the programs and commands of the microcomputers. The rockets would lift off but then fall back either directly on the spot or would fly off course. The saboteurs had either cut the wires or slackened the fuel conduits.

Learning of this sabotage, Von Braun intervened and decided the rockets should be dismantled at Mittelbau- Dora before transport and then reassembled in Blizna. This was done in the assembly hall close to the barracks near the road to Blizna.

Many local rangers or foresters from Blizna and Niwiska were also agents of the Home Army. Forest Inspector Stachowski was the leader of this close-knit group. The Germans suspected the foresters, but the amount of wood they supplied was an incredibly valuable service and resource for the Nazis. The foresters had access to virtually every location in the local heavily forested territories, and their contributions to uncovering V-weapons secrets were immense.

Fragments of rockets were readily found by the foresters and partisans, and most were covertly transported to the Allies for decoding. Sometimes, local farmers repurposed the high-grade metal into shovels and tools. The punishment for possessing one of these fragments was immediate death.

These heroic acts of sabotage came at a high price: the Nazis killed an average of 300 workers working on the missile production every day through starvation or accidents.

The story of von Braun and his men is fascinating. As the war was ending, they sought out the Americans, and von Braun's brother brokered an agreement with the US government to immigrate to America. This elite group of scientists could have chosen to work with England or the Soviet Union, so it was in America's best interests to offer them asylum.

So, it can be said that Blizna and Niwiska had a prominent role in America's space program. Out of the ashes of Nazi-occupied Europe, a group of German scientists decided to cut a deal with the Americans. Their German rocketry expertise was combined with the efforts of independent wartime scientists in California. With Werner von Braun, they carried the keys to the Space Age to America.

A V-2 newly assembled in Blizna

A Model of a V-2 at the Blizna Historical Park

ABOUT THE AUTHOR

Donna Gawell is an American author and genealogist with a passion for Polish history and culture, and most importantly, the grandmother of Colin and Elise.

Donna B Gawell's books (available on Amazon.com):

War and Resistance in the Wilderness (an adult historical novel set in the same village and time period)

Travel Back to Your Polish Roots which helps Americans learn to research their Polish genealogy, hopefully find "lost cousins," and travel to Poland to meet them.

Poland Under Nazi Rule: 1939-1941, the recently declassified CIA report written by Thaddeus Chylinski, the American Vice-Consul in Warsaw from 1920-1941.

In the Shadow of Salem is Donna's historical novel about Mehitabel Braybrooke, her 8th great grandmother who was one of the 200 accused of witchcraft during the Salem Witchcraft Trials.

The ABCs of Crime and Punishment in Puritan New England and *Travel Back to Your Roots* are non-fiction books written by the author.

Donna's website contains many articles on Polish and WWII history and traveling to Poland. She also has authored numerous history articles for professional journals and magazines.

www.DonnaGawell.com

Please leave a review of this book on Amazon.com.